S0-CJN-575

Science Behind Sports

Soccer

Science on the Pitch

By Amy B. Rogers

Portions of this book originally appeared in *Soccer* by Jenny MacKay.

Published in 2018 by
Lucent Press, an Imprint of Greenhaven Publishing, LLC
353 3rd Avenue
Suite 255
New York, NY 10010

Designer: Seth Hughes
Editor: Katie Kawa

Cataloging-in-Publication Data

Names: Rogers, Amy B.
Title: Soccer: science on the pitch / Amy B. Rogers.
Description: New York : Lucent Press, 2018. | Series: Science behind sports | Includes index.
Identifiers: ISBN 9781534561151 (library bound) | ISBN 9781534561168 (ebook)
Subjects: LCSH: Soccer–Juvenile literature.| Sports sciences–Juvenile literature.
Classification: LCC GV943.25 R64 2018 | DDC 796.334–dc23

Printed in the United States of America

CPSIA compliance information: Batch #BS17KL: For further information contact Greenhaven Publishing LLC, New York, New York at 1-844-317-7404.

Please visit our website, www.greenhavenpublishing.com. For a free color catalog of all our high-quality books, call toll free 1-844-317-7404 or fax 1-844-317-7405.

Contents

Foreword

When people watch a sporting event, they often say things such as, "That was unbelievable!" or "How could that happen?" The achievements of superstar athletes often seem humanly impossible—as if they defy the laws of nature—and all sports fans can seemingly do is admire them in awe.

However, when a person learns the science behind sports, the unbelievable becomes understandable. It no longer seems as if athletes at the top of their game are defying the laws of nature to achieve greatness; it seems as if they are using the laws of nature to their fullest potential. This kind of knowledge might be thought by some to take away from a pure appreciation of sports, but that is far from the truth. Understanding the science that makes athletic achievements possible allows fans to gain an even deeper appreciation for athletic performances and how athletes use science to their advantage.

This series introduces readers to the scientific principles behind some of the world's most popular sports. As they learn about physics concepts such as acceleration, gravity, and kinetic versus potential energy, they discover how these concepts can be applied to pitches in baseball, flips in gymnastics, dunks in basketball, and other movements in a variety of sports. In addition to the physics behind amazing plays, readers discover the science behind basic training and conditioning for different sports, the biology involved in understanding common sports injuries and their treatments, and the technological advances paving the way for the future of athletics.

The scientific concepts presented in this series are explained using accessible language and engaging examples. Complicated principles are simplified through the use of detailed diagrams, charts, graphs, and a helpful glossary. Quotations from scientists, athletes, and coaches give readers a firsthand perspective, and further research is encouraged through a detailed bibliography and a list of additional resources.

Athletes, sports fans, and budding scientists will get something important out of this series: information about how to exercise and fuel the body to excel in competition, a deeper appreciation for the history of their favorite sport, and a stronger understanding of how science works in the world around us.

The worlds of science and sports are not as far apart as they may seem. In fact, sports could not exist without science. In understanding the relationship between these two worlds, readers will become more knowledgeable sports fans and better athletes.

Chapter 1

Soccer Through the Centuries

When Americans hear the word "football," they generally think of quarterbacks, touchdowns, and passes flying through the air. However, in most other countries around the world, "football" is an entirely different sport that involves kicking the ball with the feet toward a goal. In the United States, this sport is called "soccer."

Soccer is the world's most popular sport. One of the reasons for its popularity is the ease with which it can be played. Soccer is played in big stadiums in major cities, but it is also played in open fields in developing countries. All that is really needed to play this sport is a ball (or something that can be used as a ball), an area that can serve as the goal, and people. Any open playing surface—from the most expensive turf to small patches of dirt in struggling neighborhoods—can serve as the playing field, or pitch.

Soccer has been around in various forms for thousands of years. Joseph "Sepp" Blatter, a former president of the Fédération Internationale de Football Association (FIFA)—the international governing body of professional soccer—once said, "Football is as old as the world … People have always played some form of football, from its very basic form of kicking a ball around to the game it is today."[1] Although soccer might not be quite as old as Earth itself, it has its roots in games played by ancient civilizations.

Although ancient athletes did not know it at the time, they were putting science into action every time they kicked a ball and ran across a pitch. Today's soccer players and those who work with them have a better understanding of how science factors into their performance on the pitch, and that knowledge has been used to create better equipment, training programs, and injury treatments.

Think on Your Feet!

As of 2014, 265 million people around the world play soccer. That is around 4 percent of the total global population.

Ancient Asian Games

Because the roots of soccer reach so far back into history, it is difficult to know when exactly people began playing the sport. Some of the earliest records of a kicking game that resembled soccer come from China. About 200 BC, the Chinese invented a kickball-style sport that used a round ball made of leather and stuffed with silk, fur, hair, or feathers. Players were divided into two teams, and the game was played on an area with marked edges to define the boundaries. There was a goal— a net pulled taut between two bamboo poles—in the middle of the playing area. The net had a hole about 12 inches (30 cm) wide for the ball to pass through so a team could score. Like the modern sport of soccer, players in this early Chinese ball game were able to use any body part except their hands. The sport was called *cuju* or *tsu' chu*.

Several centuries after the first records were made of *cuju*, the Japanese created their own ball-kicking game called *kemari*, which used a deerskin ball that was 9 to 10 inches (23 to 25 cm) in diameter and stuffed with sawdust. Players set out to keep the ball from touching the ground by juggling it—keeping it in the air and passing it to other players using their feet, knees, and chests but not their hands. *Kemari* games consisted of eight men, and they played within the boundaries of a field marked by specific trees in each corner—cherry, maple, willow, and pine. The sport did not pit one team against another; rather, everyone on the field worked together with the common objective of keeping the ball from touching the ground. Once a certain number of consecutive "juggles" had been accomplished, which could be up to 1,000, the game was over.

Ball-kicking games in ancient China and Japan were more than just ways for people to kill time. The games also served important purposes in their society. *Kemari* was sometimes played as part of Japanese religious ceremonies. *Cuju* was sometimes used as a form of military training and also was linked to traditional Chinese ideas and ways of thought. According to historian Nigel B. Crowther, "Ancient handbooks (including one of the earliest surviving Chinese texts) show how important *cuju* grew to be in Chinese society."[2] He has said the game was even seen to represent traditional, spiritual Chinese ideas, such as the opposite concepts of yin and yang.

Kemari is still played today by some people in Japan.

Games such as *cuju* were very symbolic in ancient cultures because they represented the world as the people understood it at the time. The field was a symbol of the earth, for example, and the ball symbolized a heavenly body such as the sun.

Early American Soccer

China and Japan were not the only cultures of the ancient world in which kickball games were important features of daily life. Similar games developed on other continents and also reflected their culture's religious and philosophical beliefs. Some of the people of ancient South America and Central America had an especially strong spiritual connection to kicking games, which may have even older origins than the games played by ancient cultures in Asia. The long history of ball games in the Americas has been demonstrated in Paso de la Amada in Mexico, where modern archaeological digs have turned up a field believed to have been used to play ball games that is estimated to be 3,500 years old. Some historians believe ball-kicking sports were played by every society in Central America. Soccer historian and author David Goldblatt has said, "The sheer number of courts and ubiquity of objects indicated that the game was played informally

Changing the Shape of Soccer

Before rubber was used to make soccer balls, the ball's shape depended on its bladder, or the part that filled with air. For a long time, the bladder in the ball was actually an animal's bladder. Then, rubber was used to make the bladder. Rubber was better than animal organs, but it had its limitations, too; it melted in hot weather and became brittle when temperatures were cold. An American inventor named Charles Goodyear was determined to find a way to make rubber weatherproof and temperature resistant, and in 1839, he found the answer. A process of treating rubber with sulfur and heating it made it retain its shape and properties in all weather conditions. Vulcanized rubber, named after Vulcan, the Roman god of fire, was born.

In 1855, Goodyear created the first soccer ball out of vulcanized rubber. This achievement was followed by the use of H. J. Lindon's inflatable rubber bladder in 1862. After these inventions, soccer balls were able to keep the round shape they have today, and they can remain durable in hot and cold weather.

by commoners as well as ritually by the elite."[3]

The ancient Maya, who lived in the rain forests of Mexico and Central America, placed extreme importance on kicking games, so much so that their beliefs about the very creation of their culture were rooted in a ball game in which two twin brothers defeated the gods and later became the sun and moon in the sky. It was not uncommon for players of Maya ball games to be sacrificed to the gods at the end of a match.

Ball games were so important to the Maya that their playing fields had phenomenal proportions. One of the world's most famous ancient landmarks is the Great Ball Court at the Maya ruins of Chichén Itzá, an archaeological site on modern-day Mexico's Yucatán Peninsula. The ball court is almost twice the size of a modern soccer field. It has a temple-like structure at either end, perhaps where ancient royalty gathered to watch important games. Despite the field's enormous size and the fact that it is open to the sky, a human whispering at one end of the court could be heard clearly by someone standing at the other end. The acoustics (physical properties that determine how sound travels) of the Great Ball Court remain a mystery, but the parallel walls along the length of the field are believed to create a "flutter echo" effect in which sound waves bounce from wall to wall to carry sounds up or down the court.

The attention paid to every small detail of the Great Ball Court, even its acoustics, shows the importance that ball-kicking games had in Maya culture and, historians believe, in nearly every other culture of Central America leading up to European colonization in the 1400s and 1500s. "In some Latin American areas soccer is simply called *pelota* (ball)—as if the only ball game existing or imaginable is soccer," author Richard Witzig wrote. "This illustrates the central cultural position soccer occupies in Latin American countries."[4]

Ball-kicking games were not just popular among the ancient Maya and other cultures of Central America. When the first English colonists arrived on the North American coast in what is now the state of Massachusetts in 1620, they wrote about Native Americans playing a ball game called *pasuckquakkohwog*, or "they gather to play ball with the foot." And when the Spanish colonized Central America and South America, they discovered something even more unique about American ball games—many American balls bounced because they were made from the sap of rubber trees native to this part of the world. Ball games played with rubber balls were far different from those played with the heavy, feather-stuffed, leather variety used elsewhere in the world.

The Great Ball Court, shown here, is a famous Maya ruin.

Evolving in Europe

Europeans, too, played various forms of ball games, borrowing elements from the ancient Greek game of *episkyros* and the ancient Roman game of *harpastum*. In *episkyros*, teams of young Greek men battled on a field to throw and kick a ball over a central line while trying to force the opposing team over its rear boundary line, which was the key to winning the game. *Harpastum* was similar to the modern-day children's game of keep-away or monkey-in-the-middle. The object was to throw and kick the ball away from someone else. Games similar to *episkyros* and *harpastum* were still played around Europe in the 19th century.

The games that eventually inspired the development of soccer were especially popular in England. In English society, sports had always been sharply divided along class lines between rich and poor. Favorite sports of the wealthy, such as hunting and polo played on horseback, differed from the favorite sports of the lower classes, such as ball-kicking games that required nothing but a ball and two teams willing to play. By the 1700s and 1800s, ball games—also known as "folk football"—among the lower classes had evolved into wildly popular and often violent matches. Entire neighboring towns sometimes battled against one another in the struggle to move the ball across the other team's goal. English ball games were officially banned by various kings at different times in history, because they were believed to threaten public safety and social order.

Then, a new tradition came about in English society—boys' schools, where upper-class young men went to live and to learn. The boys who attended these schools had few ways to spend free time because they were away from home, so they took up ball games. Schools formed teams and competed against other

Until a set of rules was established, soccer games in England were very unruly and looked quite different from the organized sport we know today.

schools. These teams quickly learned that they could not play fairly against each other without a standard set of rules, so they created ball game regulations. The groundwork of modern-day soccer as an international, organized sport was laid in the mid-1800s in the schools of England, such as Eton.

Association Rules

Early soccer games at some English schools allowed hands to be used during play, while at other schools, the use of hands was forbidden. As the schoolboys grew up, they took their favorite versions of soccer with them to the universities they attended. The debate over

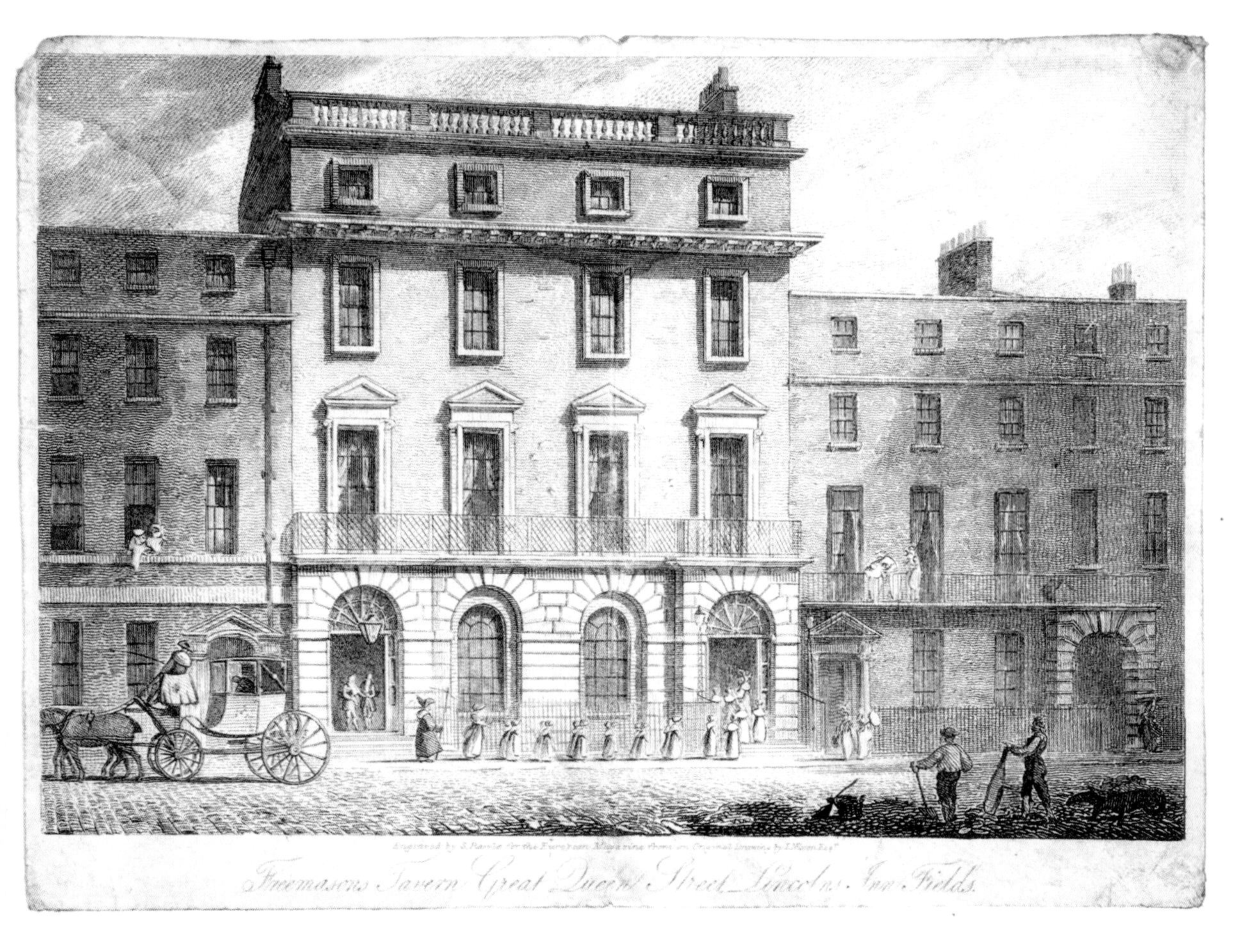

THE FREEMASON'S TAVERN, WHERE THE FOOTBALL ASSOCIATION WAS FOUNDED ON OCTOBER 26th. 1863.

The Football Association (FA) continues to serve as the governing body of English soccer, which is also known as association football.

whether hands should be used in college ball games became heated, with different schools taking different sides. The first notable attempt to standardize the rules of soccer occurred in 1846 with the establishment of the "Cambridge rules," which came from the University of Cambridge. Then, in 1863, the first official organization for the sport, the Football Association (FA), was formed in London. The members of this association wrote a set of official national rules to govern the sport.

The most controversial rule was the no-hands rule, forbidding the use of hands to touch the ball or to hold or grab other players during a game. Players who preferred the hands-on version of soccer started their own sport, rugby. Although rugby is also a popular sport, it was soccer that secured the top place in the hearts of the people of England, then Europe, then the world. Soccer became a worldwide phenomenon during the decades following that first official set of rules in 1863—rules that remain much the same in soccer today.

Think on Your Feet!

The word "soccer" was first used by the British as an abbreviation of "association football," or football played without using the hands, as opposed to "rugger," or rugby-style football, which allows players to use their hands.

The Rise of an International Pastime

Although variations of ball-kicking games had existed for several thousands of years, the "new" English version changed the world. Born during the Industrial Revolution, a period of new technology, new ideas, and new ways of living, the sport of soccer was positioned to enjoy a kind of success the human race had never before experienced in a pastime. Newspapers and telegrams became efficient ways to inform people about official rules of the new sport and to report on the outcomes of games. People in many different areas began to read about new teams and official matches in newspapers. The Industrial Revolution also brought new transportation to Europe in the form of trains, which made it possible for soccer teams to travel longer distances for games. This became increasingly important as England's fellow European countries put together their own soccer teams. Whenever there was a game to watch, local spectators flocked to the soccer field. Entire towns and cities rallied around their team on game day and squeezed in for a space in another new phenomenon—the sports stadium, built to house soccer matches and the fans who turned out in droves to watch.

Seeing an opportunity for profit, organizers of soccer teams began charging admission for spectators to see a game. The Industrial Revolution was an era of paid factory and office jobs, and many workers in England and across Europe spent money they made at their factory jobs watching soccer games. So powerful was the love of this new sport that it even changed the length of the average workweek. Since most soccer matches took place on Saturday, it became customary for employers to give their workers Saturday afternoon off in order to watch games. Before that, Saturday had been a full workday.

As soccer brought about changes to European society, the feverish love of the sport traveled across continents and oceans to reach nearly every corner of the world. Central American and South American cultures took naturally to the sport, which was not dissimilar from games they had been playing for thousands of years. Soccer is still not as popular in the United States, though, as it is in other nations around the world. However, a growing number of young people are participating in and watching soccer in the United States.

Soccer Today

Soccer has become the most-played and the most-watched sport on the planet. More of the world's nations and territories currently belong to FIFA than to the United Nations, the international organization dedicated to peace and improved standards of living worldwide. About 1.5 billion people watch one or more soccer games during a World Cup tournament, which is the most famous international tournament in soccer. Thanks to television and the Internet, approximately 1 billion people around the world watched the World Cup finals in 2014.

"It's the moment when the planet becomes a family, when we're all

Pelé's Popularity

Edson Arantes do Nascimento was born in 1940 in Brazil. He was nicknamed Pelé when he was young, and he played soccer in the dirt streets of his Brazilian hometown before becoming the sport's most famous star. Pelé played his first game for Brazil's national team when he was 16 years old, and he played in his first World Cup in 1958 at age 17. Pelé was part of teams that led Brazil to three World Cup titles (1958, 1962, and 1970).

During Pelé's 22-year career, he scored a total of 1,281 goals. He excelled at every aspect of the game, and his incredible play helped the sport of soccer grow and find new fans. Named the FIFA Player of the Century (an honor shared with Argentina's Diego Maradona), Pelé is a sports legend the world over. He will forever be known as someone who helped his sport reach new heights of popularity because of his unique skills.

Even though his professional playing days are long behind him, Pelé is still one of the most famous names in soccer.

doing the same thing whether we are in California or Nigeria or Shanghai,"[5] writer Simon Kuper said when describing the 2010 World Cup Finals.

One explanation for soccer's overwhelming worldwide popularity is that the sport is accessible to everyone. Almost anyone can learn to play soccer, whether they are male or female, large or small, muscular or graceful, old or young. This is likely an important reason why the game is popular around the world, in wealthy countries as well as in developing ones. Soccer stars can come

Women's Soccer Successes

In the United States, women's soccer did not really take off until the 1970s, with the passage of legislation called Title IX that allowed for equal athletic opportunities for male and female students in federally-funded schools. Girls and women began playing soccer in schools, and the sport then began to grow in popularity.

The United States Women's National Team (USWNT) has become a dominant force on the world soccer stage. The team won the World Cup in 1991, 1999, and 2015. It also won Olympic gold medals in 1996, 2004, 2008, and 2012. Many of the most famous and successful soccer stars of the past and present in the United States are women, including Mia Hamm, Carli Lloyd, and Abby Wambach, who, as of 2017, holds the record for most goals scored in international competition by any soccer player—male or female.

The USWNT is shown here after winning the 2015 World Cup.

from anywhere and from any walk of life, and it has had a universal appeal since its earliest days. It is, as Witzig said, "almost as if the human collective consciousness willed the game of soccer into being."[6]

Soccer was not simply willed into being, however. It is a combination of various scientific factors at work—from the forces needed to kick the ball into the goal to the body systems that must work together to allow players to perform at their best. Long before people understood the science behind soccer, those factors were still working to make matches exciting. As the sport has evolved, so has fans' understanding of the role of science in every moment of a soccer match. That understanding has helped fans gain a deeper appreciation for what soccer players have been able to accomplish throughout the history of the sport.

Chapter 2

Physics on the Pitch

Every moment of a soccer match is a mini physics lesson. Physics is the science of matter and energy and how they interact, and there is plenty of both matter and energy on display in a soccer match. The act of kicking the ball to another player or toward the goal might not seem particularly complex, but many physics concepts can be seen in that one action. The physical properties of the ball, the energy used to kick it, the forces that keep it moving toward its target, and the way the field itself works to speed up or slow down the movement of the ball are all examples of physics in action.

Some critics complain that soccer matches do not have enough exciting moments. However, if you understand the physics behind the sport and pay attention to how it plays out on the pitch, each second of a match is action-packed.

By the Numbers

Soccer requires a standard set of regulations so that everyone plays by the same rules and opponents have an equal chance of winning. One thing official rules specify is the size of the rectangular soccer pitch. The perimeter, or the outer edge of the field, is marked with white lines. There is a goal box at the center point of each short end of the field, with a penalty area marked in front of the goal box. A centerline is also marked across the exact middle of the field. Many soccer rules, such as whether the ball can remain in play or has gone out of bounds and where players can stand during a penalty kick, depend on these lines. A typical soccer field for adult players is about 75 yards (69 m) wide by 120 yards (110 m) long, which is slightly larger than the size of an American football field.

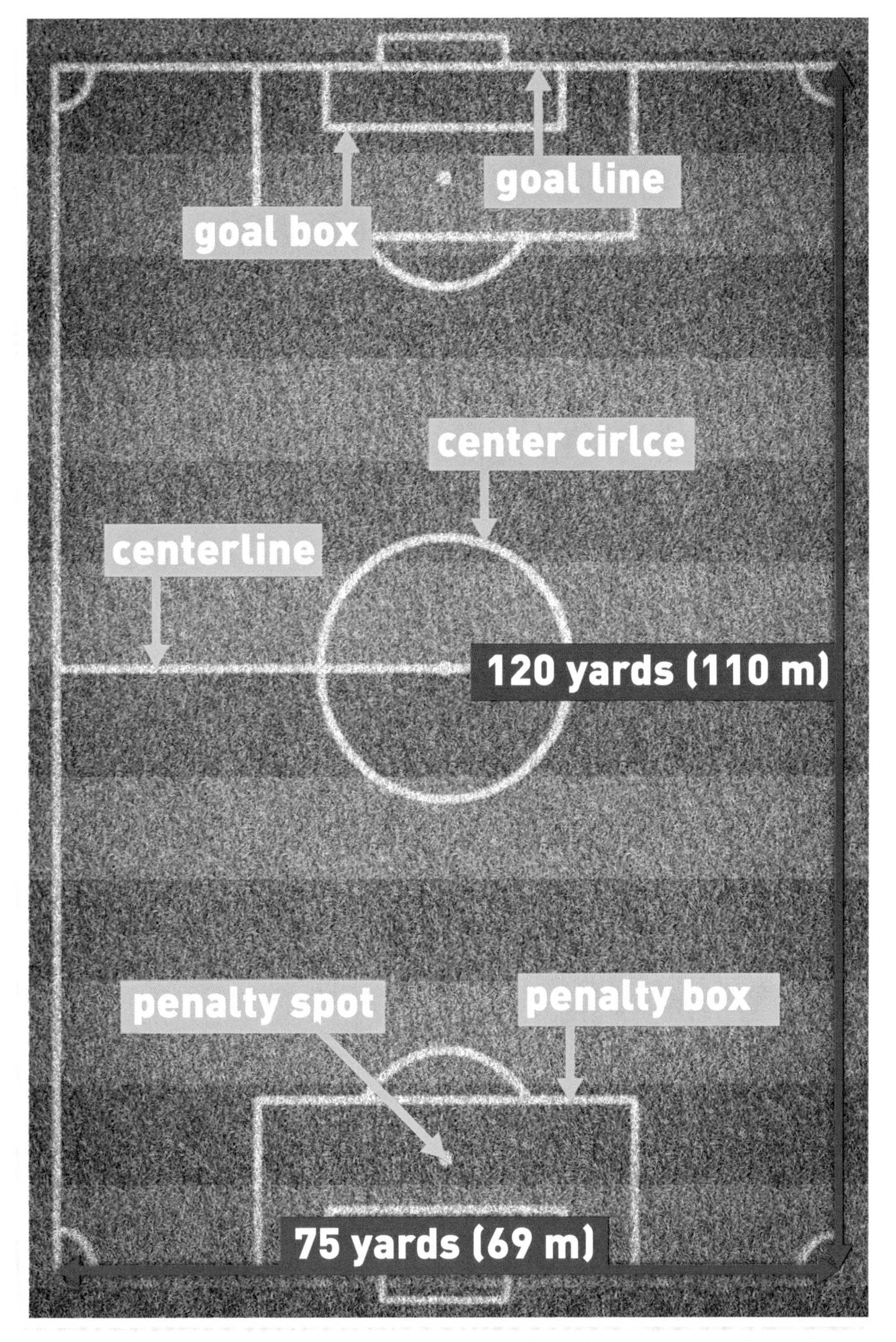

If the sides of a soccer pitch measure 75 yards (69 m) by 120 yards (110 m), its area is 9,000 square yards (7,590 sq m). Area is found by multiplying a rectangle's length by its width.

In an official soccer match, two teams of eleven players face off. One player on each team is the goalkeeper, who attempts to keep the ball out of the goal, preventing the other team from scoring. The goalkeeper, or goalie, can use their hands. With a total of 22 players moving on the field at one time, the field's dimensions are extremely important. "There must be a general relation between the number of players and the best size of the pitch," author John Wesson said. He continued,

> *The essential factor is that there be pressure on the players to quickly control the ball and decide what to do with it. This means that opposing players must typically be able to run to the player with the ball in a time comparable with the time taken to receive, control, and move the ball. If the distance between players is larger, the game loses tension. If the distance is much less the game has the appearance of a pinball machine.*[7]

The size of an official soccer field and the number of players per team were not chosen at random. A field's dimensions give both teams a fair chance at stealing the ball from each other and at passing it effectively among their teammates. The field's size helps determine how players position themselves within it. They must gauge how fast the ball can travel, for example, and what trajectory the ball will take—whether it will rise over the heads of players or drop quickly to the ground. These details, governed by physics, determine whether and how fast a soccer ball will reach its intended recipient during a pass without rolling out of bounds.

Newton's Laws in Action

Resting objects, such as soccer balls, stay still if no force acts on them, and whenever a certain amount of force is applied to a resting object, it moves with predictable force. These phenomena were first described in the late 1600s by an English physicist named Isaac Newton, who described the behavior of any moving object with three simple statements, now known as Newton's laws of motion.

Newton's first law of motion states that a moving object will stay in motion at the same speed, in a straight line, until another force acts on it to change its velocity, or the rate at which it changes position. His second law states that there is a relationship between the mass of an object and the amount of force that must be applied in order to move it at a specific velocity. The third law of motion states that for every action, such as kicking a soccer ball, there is an equal and opposite reaction.

Newton's three laws are some of the most important facts in physics—and soccer games. Knowing that the velocity at which a resting object will move depends on the force applied to it, soccer players plan the force of their kicks to control the ball, keep it away from

Soccer players must understand the relationship between the force of their kick and the velocity at which the ball moves to complete successful passes and shots on goal. This means they must understand Newton's three laws of motion.

the other team, and move toward the other team's goal. They use knowledge of physics—what the ball will do once it is in motion—to position themselves close enough to or far enough from their teammates and opponents to have the best chance of completing, receiving, and intercepting passes. They also understand that any action, such as intercepting a ball, will cause an opposite reaction—a ball that hits a solid surface will naturally bounce the other way.

According to Newton's first law of motion, a resting soccer ball will not move until someone kicks it, and the direction and strength of the kick are essential. If a kick is too hard, the ball will sail over the players' heads and out of bounds. If a kick is too soft, it will move slowly, giving the other team an opportunity to dash in and steal it. Skilled soccer players have learned to kick with just the right amount of force. They must use their muscles to harness a certain amount of energy, which is then passed to a soccer ball during a kick to set it in motion.

Think on Your Feet!

Newton's first law of motion is sometimes called the law of inertia because inertia is the resistance an object has to a change in motion.

Measuring Motion

Soccer players are often in motion around the pitch—running toward the goal, running to break up a pass, or moving to stop a shot. However, not all motion in a soccer game is the same, so it needs to be measured differently.

Speed measures the rate at which something moves. The direction an object moves does not matter when measuring speed. For example, soccer players can show speed when they run, even if they end up back where they started on the field. On the other hand, velocity measures the rate at which something changes its position, so the direction of movement matters. To show velocity, an object needs to move away from where it started. A soccer player can show this by running down the field to score a goal.

Acceleration is another way motion is measured. It is the measurement of how much an object's velocity changes over time. When velocity increases, the object is said to be accelerating. A soccer player accelerates when they increase their velocity to move faster than the defenders around them to reach the goal.

Factoring in Forces

Soccer players also adapt their kicks and their awareness of where the ball is and where it is going to accommodate for gravity, or the pull of Earth on other objects. All objects have gravity—a force that pulls all matter together. The more mass an object contains, the stronger the pull of gravity. Because Earth contains much more mass than any person or object on it, the planet exerts a force of gravity that pulls smaller things on its surface down toward it.

The force of gravity counteracts an object's tendency to stay in motion in a straight line. When a soccer ball sails into the air, there is a point at which it can rise no farther; the pull of Earth's gravity overcomes the ball's upward motion and starts bringing it back down to the ground. Gravity is what makes a ball move in an arc after a hard kick—it rises, and then it begins to come back down to Earth. Experienced soccer players can predict when and where the ball will descend, positioning themselves

When designing a soccer field, people must take into account how the force of friction from the grass, or turf, will affect the movement of the ball and the players. Friction also exists between the soccer players' shoes and the ground. Too much friction will slow them down, but not enough will cause them to slip and possibly fall. This is why soccer players wear cleats; the shoes create more friction.

near the point where it will come back down so they can try to intercept it.

A soccer ball's trajectory can also be affected by environmental forces, such as wind. If wind and the ball are moving in opposite directions, then the blowing wind will create a force of resistance against the ball. In short, the ball will not go as far unless a player kicks harder to compensate for the force of the wind. Even balls kicked along the ground are subject to resistance in the form of friction, which is a force created whenever two surfaces rub or slide against each other. Soccer balls experience friction when they roll or bounce along the ground, especially on surfaces such as the grass of the playing field. Long grass, which has more surface area, will create more friction, absorb more of the ball's energy, and slow the ball down faster than short grass will.

A soccer player is constantly considering basic facts of physics, such as the laws of motion, gravity's pull on the ball, wind resistance, and friction, throughout a game. "Does the player use physics formulas? Of course not," engineers Seyed Hamid Hamraz and Seyed Shams Feyzabadi have said. However, they added, "We can firmly express that the player [learns] by way of experience."[8] A soccer player's actions are anything but random. They are guided by an innate understanding of physics, mastered through practice.

Bending It Like Beckham

David Beckham was a famous soccer player known for his skill at "bending" a soccer ball's trajectory around players to score. This skill actually has a scientific name: the Magnus effect. The Magnus effect is caused by changes in velocity as an object moves through a liquid or gas, such as air. In soccer, the Magnus effect can be seen when a spinning soccer ball moves through the air. The resistance, or drag, caused by the air around the ball slows the movement of the air on one side of the ball and speeds up the air's movement on the opposite side. This causes a difference in air pressure, and the ball's trajectory bends toward the lower air pressure on the side where the air is moving faster. The way a soccer ball's path curves when the Magnus effect is at work is commonly called a "banana kick" because the trajectory is curved like a banana.

The Magnus effect is seen in many other sports, too. If a ball is spinning through the air, you'll be able to see the Magnus effect in action. In baseball, the Magnus effect is the reason curveball pitches curve. Golfers use the Magnus effect to bend their shots around things that are in their way, such as trees.

David Beckham was known for his ability to score amazing goals that seemed to bend around other players. It might have looked like magic to some, but it was actually the Magnus effect in action.

Size and Scoring

Whether a ball will overcome gravity, friction, and the actions of other players to make it into the goal is the big question in soccer. Like the size of the soccer field, the size of the goal boxes is important to the outcome of a soccer match. A standard goal in an adult soccer game is a metal frame 24 feet (7.3 m) wide by 8 feet (2.4 m) tall. These dimensions give the goalkeeper a fair chance at defending the entire goal and the opposing team a fair chance at getting the ball past the goalkeeper and scoring.

The best goalkeepers and goal scorers in the world are fairly evenly matched. "A top-class goalkeeper can cover the whole of the goal given a little more

Goalkeepers have to be quick, both mentally and physically, to cover the necessary ground to stop the ball from going into the goal.

Think on Your Feet!

More than 3 million children play organized soccer in the United States.

than a second," Wesson explained, and a good kicker "can kick the ball at 80 miles [129 km] per hour."[9] This is why the dimensions of the goal were carefully chosen to ensure that neither the player trying to score nor the player trying to stop them had too much of an advantage. A larger goal would be too difficult for a goalkeeper to defend, making goals too easy to score. A smaller goal would make it almost impossible for the opposing team to score. Specific dimensions for the goal box help make a soccer game fair for both teams.

An Even Playing Field

There is more to a balanced soccer field than standard measurements and dimensions. To make sure a match is fair, fields must be literally balanced, meaning that they do not slope from one end to the other. They also cannot have hills, dips, or craters. An uneven field can make the game more difficult for one team than the other. It can also lead to added risk of injuries for the players.

People who design competitive sports fields use physics to create level playing surfaces that are safe and fair for both teams. First, the area must be mostly flat. A field cannot slope noticeably from side to side, because a slope will affect the movement of the soccer ball. A ball that lands on a flat surface will stay put, but a ball that lands on a slope will begin to roll down the slope due to the force of gravity, and this will affect everything about how the soccer game is played. The ball may go out of bounds more often, for example, if the field is sloped in a way that makes it roll outside the perimeter line of the field. Every time a ball goes out of bounds, play must stop while a player throws the ball back in. This interrupts the flow of the game and is frustrating for players and spectators.

Even worse than a field that slopes from side to side is one that slopes from end to end. The team whose goal is on the downhill end of the slope will be at a distinct disadvantage. The players will constantly be fighting the ball's tendency to roll toward their own goal. They will also have to run uphill against the slope as they try to move the ball toward the opposing team's goal. This requires more energy than running on a flat field. The players on the opposite team, meanwhile, will be working downhill; the ball will naturally roll in their favor, and it will take less physical effort to run toward the opposing team's goal. Even a slight slope, invisible to the naked eye, can make a difference in the efforts of the two teams and in the outcome of a game. The people who design soccer fields carefully measure for any slope in the area where they want to build a field. If the field is sloped, dirt must be added or removed to level the area.

Think on Your Feet!

A soccer player can run for as many as 7 miles (11.2 km) during a match.

Watch Out for Water!

Just as important as removing a noticeable slope from the field is smoothing out any sudden hills or dips. A soccer player running at full speed and concentrating on other players and the ball may not see an uneven patch of ground and might stumble or trip. Not only will this interrupt the momentum of the game, but a player could also be injured. Therefore, field designers take extra care to make sure that a soccer field is without any uneven areas, such as bumps or craters.

Perfectly flat fields, however, can also pose problems. The physical properties of water and its tendency to puddle can have an effect on the outcome of a soccer game, too. Water that falls on a soccer field during a rainstorm or from sprinklers watering the grass will have nowhere to go. It will form puddles or sheets of water, and these make their own hazards during a soccer game. Water molecules have a tendency to stick to one another, which is why water molecules form water droplets and why water droplets group together to form puddles. Whenever a ball rolls through a puddle, water droplets stick to it, and this can create problems in a game. The surface of a wet ball that has absorbed a small amount of water is slicker and slightly heavier than that of a dry ball, and this could affect the players' handling of it. Still another problem with wet fields is that if soccer players step into puddles or soggy areas, they might slip, lose their footing, or miss an important pass or kick. This is because the water acts as a lubricant, or a substance

Soccer fields, especially professional pitches, must be carefully designed to be as safe as possible.

that reduces friction. The reduced friction between a player's feet and the turf can be dangerous. "Each time a soccer player kicks the ball, he or she is by definition standing on one foot in a posture that requires good footing," Jim Puhalla, Jeff Krans, and Mike Goatley wrote in their manual for designing sports fields. "So evenness of the surface becomes an increasingly important issue for the safety and performance of the athletes."[10]

To prevent water from collecting on soccer fields, architects design the fields to avoid water buildup. They most often

Under Pressure

When a soccer ball is filled with air, it is actually being filled with many individual air molecules. Although air is invisible, it still has weight and takes up space. When many air molecules come together, they take up more space and begin to press against an object or surface. The force of this pressing is called air pressure. Air pressure is created in a container when air molecules get crammed together in one place. A soccer ball is a container because its bladder holds air. The air pressure inside the ball increases as more air is pumped into the ball.

A soccer ball must be filled with the right amount of air or it will not perform as expected. Air pressure affects an object's elasticity, or its ability to return to its normal shape after an outside force has attempted to change that shape. Lower air pressure means lower elasticity, so a soccer ball that is underinflated will not return to its original shape after being kicked. On the other hand, if a soccer ball is inflated with too much air, its bladder might break from the air pressure being too great for the container.

do this by adding an almost unnoticeable hill, or crown, down the center of the field lengthwise. This makes the field slope very slightly at a grade of about 1 to 2 percent from the center toward both sidelines. In other words, for every 12 inches (30 cm) of distance across the field from the center crown, the field will slope down about 0.25 inch (0.64 cm). With this slight slope, any water that collects on the field will trickle toward the sidelines instead of forming puddles on the playing surface. It is important that the slope is not enough to affect the rolling of the ball or the running of the players. This is why the people who design soccer fields need to have a strong understanding of physics and math to do their job successfully.

Soccer Ball Basics

The laws of physics do not just affect the way architects design playing fields. Physics properties are also critical to the key component of the game—the ball. A soccer ball is in nearly constant motion during a match as it is kicked, nudged, bumped off of heads, and caught by the goalkeeper. The ball's physical properties are designed specifically for the different ways it is put to use during a match.

The dimensions of soccer balls have changed little since the first official soccer rules were written in the late 1800s. Players realized that there is an optimal size and weight for a ball. Balls that are too heavy require too much strength to kick, and a heavy ball may cause head or neck injuries if a player uses her head to stop and redirect it. A ball that is too light, on the other hand, may not travel as players expect. It is much more vulnerable to wind resistance on a blustery day, for example. Bowling balls would be too heavy for use in a soccer game, and beach balls would not be heavy enough. These examples demonstrate why mass (the amount of matter within an object of a certain size) and weight (the amount of gravitational pull Earth has on an object due to its mass) are important characteristics for a soccer ball. Even slight differences in size or weight can change the way a ball travels across the ground or through the air and could make a pass fall short of its target or a shot fly wide of the goal.

A standard soccer ball for adults is generally between 14 and 16 ounces (397 and 454 g), and its circumference—the distance around the circular shape—is generally between 27 and 28 inches (69 and 71 cm). These specifications are important because players expect a standard soccer ball to behave a certain way when kicked, dribbled, or bounced off the head. Similar to a field that has not been designed according to official regulations, a ball that has not been made according to official dimensions may change the flow or even the entire outcome of a game because it does not behave in a scientifically predictable way.

The shape of a soccer ball also needs to remain standardized to allow the game to play out in a safe, relatively predictable way. Because it is a ball, people often mistakenly say that it is a sphere. However, a soccer ball is actually a shape known as a truncated icosahedron. This is a shape with 60 vertices, or points. Soccer balls commonly have 12 pentagonal, or five-sided, faces and 20 hexagonal, or six-sided, faces. Each face is stitched or glued on as its own patch, or panel. On a traditional soccer ball, the pentagonal faces are black, and the hexagonal faces are white. The faces are curved, so the ball has a shape close to a sphere without being perfectly spherical.

Although this design is the most common, it is not necessarily the best. Scientists and engineers are still working to determine the most aerodynamic shape for a soccer ball. Aerodynamics is the branch of science that deals with the way air moves around objects and the way objects move through the air. Soccer balls need to be aerodynamic in order to move easily through the air toward the goal or to another player. Scientists conduct tests and experiments to see how changes in a soccer ball's design affect its aerodynamics.

Because of these tests, different soccer balls have been used at World Cup events in recent years. These balls were made from a decreasing number of panels. What started as 32 became

14 panels in 2006 and then 8 panels in 2010. In 2014, the Brazuca soccer ball was introduced at the World Cup in Brazil. This ball was made with only six panels. The people who designed it believed its identical panels provided the best possible stability and made for the most aerodynamic ball.

The Brazuca soccer ball used in the 2014 World Cup is shown here. It went through many scientific tests before it was put to use on the pitch.

Putting Things in Motion

The dimensions of the field, the size of the goal boxes, and the design of the ball are all critical to the outcome of a soccer match. All of these elements have scientific reasons behind their shape, size, and construction. Physics plays an important role in a soccer match, and soccer equipment and fields are designed with physics in mind.

The truly essential components of a soccer game, however, are the people playing it. The field, the goal, and the ball mean nothing without players. The players put the ball in motion using force. The players turn potential, or stored, energy into kinetic energy, or energy in motion. The players take the physics concepts and put them into practice using their body, giving spectators a sporting event and a science lesson to enjoy.

Chapter 3

The Mechanics of Movement

The greatest soccer players often look like unstoppable machines on the pitch. That was certainly the case at the 2015 Women's World Cup, when American Carli Lloyd scored a hat trick—three goals—in just 16 minutes, helping her team beat Japan, 5–2, in the final. A hat trick is rare in any soccer game, but to do it on the sport's biggest stage and in such a short amount of time made Lloyd appear superhuman, which fit her nickname, "Captain America."

Each of Lloyd's three goals was impressive, but perhaps the most incredible of them all was her third goal, which was a shot from the centerline that somehow made its way past the Japanese goalkeeper and into the net. As Nate Scott wrote in *USA Today*, "It didn't make any sense. It shouldn't have worked. But it worked."[11]

How did it work? A variety of scientific factors were at work, allowing Lloyd to send the ball flying through the air, behind the goalkeeper, and into the history books. Her ability to accelerate past defenders, keep her balance, and get just the right amount of force behind her kick can all be explained using biomechanics, or the science of movement.

The study of biomechanics aims to explain the body and its actions as the workings of a living machine. This is certainly true for superstar soccer players such as Lloyd, whose bodies are some of the most finely-tuned machines in the world. A soccer player's body features many parts that work together to achieve athletic greatness. What might look simple to fans watching from their seat is often anything but simple when looked at from a scientific perspective.

Carli Lloyd's hat trick at the 2015 Women's World Cup was an amazing athletic achievement and a biomechanical marvel.

Even the most basic soccer skills—running, kicking, and stopping the ball—cannot be executed without the player's body parts working in the correct way at the correct time.

Think on Your Feet!

The first FIFA Women's World Cup was played in 1991, 61 years after the first Men's World Cup was played.

Using Legs as Levers

Soccer is mostly a kicking game, a sport dominated by the work of the legs and feet. It is called football in most countries of the world for a good reason—the foot is what comes in contact most often with the ball. However, in terms of mechanics, the foot is merely the end of the leg. With every kick of the ball, the foot functions like the snapping tip of a whip, but the whip itself—the entire leg—drives every kick.

In soccer, the human leg works as a system of levers—straight bars that rotate or pivot around a fixed point, or fulcrum, to apply force to another point (in this case, the ball). The straight bones of the leg—the femur in the thigh and the tibia and fibula that make up the shin—act as the bars of the lever. The fulcrums are the joints—the hip, knee, and ankle. Both portions of the leg—upper and lower—act as separate but related levers during a kick, combining their force and direction to make the foot connect with the ball with particular power or precision. Because the hip joint can rotate, it can move the upper leg not just backward and forward but diagonally and from side to side. The knee joint moves only forward and backward, but combined with the variety of angles possible at the hip, both joints work together to create a lever that can make contact with the ball from limitless directions and with various amounts of force. This force that is applied to the ball is fittingly known as applied force.

Controlling the direction and force of the leg and foot at the moment of a kick is the central skill of soccer. The velocity of the ball is related to the force used to move it—the strength of the kick. A good soccer player at the professional level has the ability to kick the ball an average of 98 feet (29 m) per second, but kicking that hard is not always an advantage. A ball that sails past its intended target—a teammate or the goal—does no good to anyone in a soccer game. Most soccer kicks, in fact, are designed to achieve a velocity that is well below what powerful kickers could achieve if they gave it their all. Often just a mere tap of the ball is needed, such as when players dribble, making short kicks to keep the ball in front of them as they run up the field. Soccer players need to understand how to use their legs as effective levers to apply just the right amount of force to the ball.

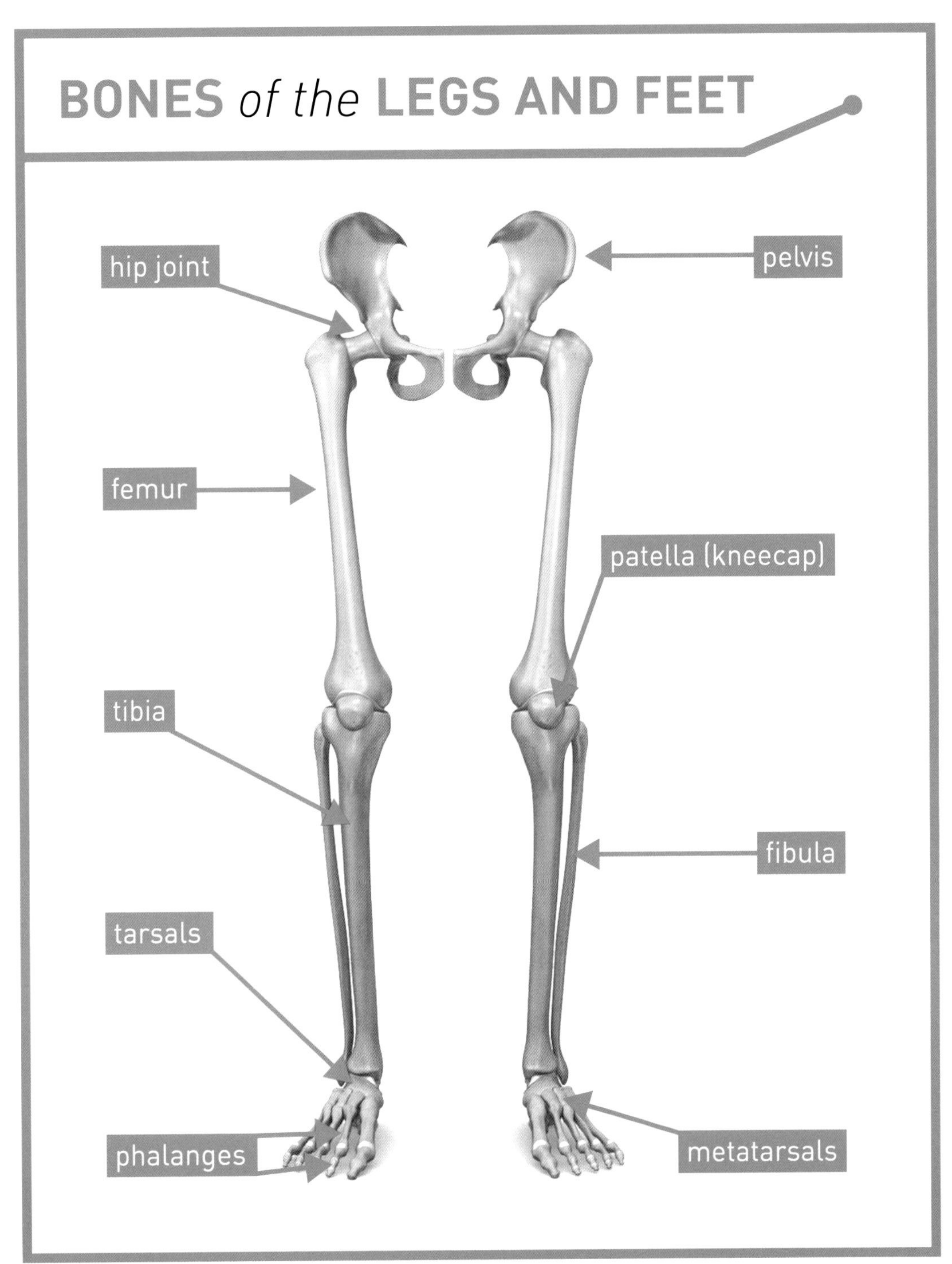

All the bones in the leg and foot work together to apply force to a soccer ball.

Think on Your Feet!

There are 26 bones in each human foot.

Muscles in Motion

A soccer player's ability to apply just the right amount of force to the ball is controlled by muscles. Muscles are attached to and control the movement of bones, which in the case of kicking, means the direction and force of the lever system created by the legs. The quadriceps is the large muscle running down the front of the thigh. Along the back of the thigh are the hamstrings, and where the femur bone of the thigh connects to the hip are the hip flexor muscles. These are the major muscles responsible for moving the leg in a soccer kick.

The biomechanical action of a full-force kick happens in this way: First, the soccer player plants one foot on the ground as support. This frees up the opposite leg to work as the kicking lever. The player then extends the kicking leg as far back as necessary; the larger the swing of the lever, the more energy the foot can transfer to the ball and the more forceful the kick will be. Once the leg is extended backward, the hip flexor muscle at the front of the hip tenses to pull the thigh forward. When the knee is positioned over the ball, the hamstring muscle along the back of the thigh, which has been tensed to pull the lower leg backward, releases its tension. The powerful quadriceps, meanwhile, tenses to pull the lower leg and the foot forward. The shin swings down like a whip, and the foot, which is anchored by a stiff ankle so it works like the heavy end of a club, transfers the combined energy of the entire leg to its target, the ball.

Breaking Down the Best Kicks

Soccer players do not typically kick the ball with the top of the foot or their toes. This way of kicking gives them too little control over the ball's direction. Instead, they kick with their instep, which is the side of their foot. The instep has a greater surface area than the toe, which gives the player more control over where the ball is going.

Most soccer kicks also start from the side of the ball rather than from directly behind it. This is because approaching the ball from the side allows the soccer player's hip to rotate more than it could from a position directly behind the ball. Hip rotation allows for more force to be applied to the ball, which makes for a stronger kick.

The kick works like a chain reaction, gathering strength and momentum from the start of the backswing to the instant of impact, when the energy of the leg is transferred to the ball to set it in motion. The kick is the most familiar biomechanical application in the game of soccer.

The Science of Trapping

Kicking is the main action most people associate with soccer, but stopping the movement of a ball that has been kicked is just as important, because it allows players to intercept passes or keep the ball out of the goal. Stopping a moving soccer ball is known as trapping, and it involves different biomechanical principles than kicking. The kick involves transferring energy to the ball to make it move, but the trap involves absorbing a moving ball's energy to slow it down.

Newton's first and second laws of motion state that a resting object stays still unless a force moves it, and whenever a certain amount of force is applied to an object, it will move predictably. Both are important concepts for soccer players, since they are the reason a soccer ball must be kicked with a certain amount of force in order for it to move the way players want. Newton's third law of motion is also very important in soccer. This law states that for every action, there is an equal and opposite reaction. Actions and reactions always occur in equal pairs. Whenever a moving soccer ball hits a solid surface, for example, the ball exerts a force on the surface at the moment of impact. The surface also exerts its own equal force back against the ball.

This concept of opposite reactions is critical in soccer, because when players are not dribbling or passing the ball, they are generally trying to trap it, placing themselves in front of it to stop its progress and make it fall to their feet so they can control it. Since no soccer player other than the goalie can use hands to catch the ball, stopping the ball's progress means placing some part of the body—the chest, the knee, the foot, the thigh, or even the head—directly in the path of the moving ball. However, Newton's third law of motion predicts that when a moving ball strikes another object, such as a human leg or torso, the ball will tend to bounce off and move the other way. To effectively trap a soccer ball and keep control of it, soccer players use special techniques to counteract Newton's third law of motion.

The trick to successfully trapping a moving ball is to absorb its energy. A soccer ball will not bounce off a flexible surface, such as a pillow, the same way it will bounce off a hard surface, such as a brick wall. At the moment of impact, the flexible surface will move a little in the direction the ball is already going. The surface acts as a cushion, sinking in slightly to absorb some of the ball's force when the two objects collide. This will reduce the ball's tendency to bounce the opposite way. The wall, on the other

Trapping the ball is an important soccer skill, so it is important for soccer players to understand the science behind it, including Newton's third law of motion and the ways kinetic energy—energy of motion—is absorbed.

An Energetic Sport

There are two main kinds of energy, and both can be seen in a soccer match. Potential energy is the energy an object has because of its position. It is also known as stored energy. A soccer ball that has been trapped and is sitting at a player's feet has potential energy. The second kind of energy is kinetic energy, or energy of motion. An object has kinetic energy when it is moving. When a soccer ball is kicked after it has been trapped, it has kinetic energy.

The law of conservation of energy states that energy cannot be created or destroyed. It can only change forms. Therefore, when soccer players trap the ball, they are not removing energy, they are simply absorbing it. Kinetic energy becomes potential energy; it does not disappear. In the same way, when soccer players kick the ball, they are not creating new energy. The potential energy in the ball is being changed into kinetic energy by the force of the kick.

hand, will not flex at the moment of collision. It will not cushion the impact or absorb the ball's energy, so the ball's movement in the opposite direction after the impact will be greater. To trap a ball, then, soccer players must try to cushion it—to absorb some of the moving ball's energy at the moment of impact. They do this by allowing their chest, thigh, knee, foot, or other body part to move a little in the same direction the ball is already going. This way, when the ball connects with a player's body, most of its energy is absorbed, not deflected. The ball will drop to the ground near the player's feet and remain in their possession instead of bouncing away toward opponents who could steal it. This makes the trap an essential technique for soccer players to master.

Staying Low

To effectively trap a soccer ball by moving in the direction it is already going, the body's center of gravity becomes important. Every object has a center of gravity, or single point at which the bulk of its weight is concentrated. The motion of any object can be described as the motion of its center of gravity from one place to another. Objects also turn or rotate around their center of gravity. When soccer players attempt to trap a ball, they not only have to gauge the ball's center of gravity to understand its motion, they must also understand their own center of gravity—how and where they need to position themselves so they can absorb the force of the ball without being thrown off balance.

Women have a lower center of gravity than men. This is because more of a woman's body mass is concentrated in her lower body.

Center of gravity is closely tied to balance. Objects with a low center of gravity have their center point of weight positioned close to the ground—in general, these are broader, flatter objects that would be difficult to knock over. The higher the center of gravity, the easier it is for an object to topple. Young trees are a good example of how the center of gravity works. If a tree is tall and wispy, its center of gravity is higher off the ground. A strong wind will cause it to bend or even break. However, if the tree is short and solid, its center of gravity is low to the ground, and it is less likely to bend in the wind. Even if the two trees have the exact same weight and mass, the one with the lower center of gravity will be more difficult to knock over.

Soccer players use the same concept during a game, especially when they trap a ball. They may bend their knees slightly to lower their center of gravity so they can absorb the ball's impact with their body. If their center of gravity is too high, a forcefully kicked ball might knock them off balance when they try to trap it. Good soccer players have an innate understanding of their center of gravity and use it to their advantage on the field, helping them to move side to side to trap a ball or to change direction in an instant. "Athletes that need to be able to turn quickly know to keep their center of gravity low,"[12] civil engineer Cameron Bauer has stated. By keeping their center of gravity low, players are better able to change direction while maintaining their balance. Center of gravity is one of the most important elements of biomechanics in soccer.

Using Their Head

Soccer players also use their center of gravity to help make up for the fact that they cannot use their hands. Instead, they fine-tune their ability to move their entire body toward a ball to stop or redirect its progress. One of the most unique skills in soccer is the use of the head to stop or move the ball. Like the act of kicking, where the weakest part of the leg—the foot—is what makes contact with the ball, the act of heading transfers force from a stronger part of the body—the trunk, made up of the back and chest—up through the neck to the striking point, which is the forehead. Often, the player jumps into the air to make contact with the ball, which means additional force is coming from the lower body, including the knees and hip flexors. The point of a header is not to have the ball hit the player in the head, but to have the player actively meet the ball in the air. The knees are bent and the torso is angled down when a player is in the proper position to execute a header. This keeps their center of gravity closer to the ground to maintain their balance and achieve maximum force to help redirect the force of the ball.

A strong understanding of biomechanics helps soccer players avoid injury when heading the ball.

Using the head as a primary striking force seems as if it would cause serious injury, but heading is relatively safe because players train themselves to contract their neck muscles so that the neck and head themselves are not whipped forward but act as a stiff, clubbing surface. In addition, the use of the forehead helps remove some injury risk because that is a thicker part of the skull, which allows for better absorption of energy and force.

No Hands?

Although soccer is known for the fact that players generally cannot use their hands during a match, it is not a game played without any use of hands whatsoever. The rules state that hands and arms cannot be used by players other than the goalkeeper to catch the ball, change its direction, or push or grab other players. However, when soccer players are in action on the field, their hands and arms do not remain stiffly at their sides. Even though the arms do not actually touch the ball, they are used in almost every kick, header, and jump in the game. For one thing, arms held out to the sides help balance the body around its center of gravity, because having an equal amount of weight on both sides of the torso makes it more difficult for gravity to topple a person over. This is why it is easier for gymnasts to walk along a balance beam with their arms lifted away from the body and why arms held out to the sides act as a balancing mechanism when a soccer player is preparing to kick the ball. The arms are used in soccer during headers, too. They help players keep their balance, and when swung in a front-to-back motion, the arms add momentum and force to the forward motion of the torso during a header.

Whenever the ball rolls out of bounds in a soccer game, hands are important, too. A game stops momentarily while a player throws the ball back into play, often by gripping the ball with both hands, bringing the arms back over the head, and flinging the ball back onto the field. A properly executed throw-in is often critical to a successful soccer game. "Restarts, or dead-ball situations, provide some of the best opportunities in soccer to create goal-scoring chances,"[13] soccer coach Gene Klein stated. At the same time, a botched toss from the sidelines can be intercepted by the opposing team, leading to a score. "Players need to realize games can be won or lost in these situations,"[14] Klein added. Understanding the biomechanics of arm movements can help players execute a successful throw-in. Like the leg, the arm also acts as a lever, with the joints around it—the elbow, shoulder, and wrist—serving as fulcrums. The position of the arms and the amount of force they exert can help determine where the ball will land on a throw-in.

Nowhere on the soccer field are hands as important, however, as in the goal box. The goalkeeper is the one player on a soccer team allowed to use any part of the body that will help keep the ball out of the goal. The goalkeeper may kick, trap, and even head a ball if that is the best way to stop the other team from scoring. Goalkeepers are known for their ability to leap, dive, and tumble to catch the ball. They do this by instantaneously using principles of biomechanics and laws of motion. "Top goalkeepers have what we call *soft hands*," former soccer players Peter Mellor and Tony Waiters wrote. "They seem to be able to absorb the ball."[15] Goalkeepers do not technically absorb the ball, but they are able to keep it from bouncing off their hands by applying the principles of physics and biomechanics to their actions. They do not stiffen their hands completely; they allow for some flexibility when the ball touches them. This allows them to absorb some of the force of impact from the ball. Then, they are able to hold onto the ball instead of the ball bouncing off their hands—according to Newton's third law—and back into play.

Goalkeepers often wear gloves to create more friction between their hands and the ball, making it less likely that the ball will slip out of their grasp.

Becoming Finely-Tuned Machines

It may seem as though soccer players have a natural ability to make the most of biomechanical principles and physics on the pitch. To some degree, that may be true. However, most soccer players work very hard to achieve what looks like an effortless combination of skill and science. They train for long hours and condition their bodies to perform at their best. This training also requires a strong understanding of science to help athletes safely and successfully master the sport of soccer. If soccer players often seem to behave like finely-tuned machines, it is a result of years of tough training.

Chapter 4

Training to Be the Best

Soccer is a game that is played by people around the world who represent different ages, skill levels, and body types. As Richard Witzig has stated, "There is no perfect soccer body."[16] However, the best soccer players work hard to be in the best physical condition. Soccer—especially when played at its highest level—is a sport that demands a lot from the body. Soccer players need to develop the endurance required to run many miles during a game. They also need to develop the physical strength to power their kicks and sprint toward the ball or the goal, as well as the balance and coordination necessary to trap or head the ball.

Soccer players develop these physical abilities through long hours of training and conditioning. Their coaches often help them develop training programs that focus on specific body parts and skills. In some cases, soccer players have trainers who help them get their body in the best physical shape for peak performance on the pitch. Coaches, trainers, and players put careful thought into creating the right training programs and practice schedules. They take into account scientific principles, including biomechanical principles, and use their knowledge of the human body to ensure that each exercise has a specific purpose and is done safely.

Proper training is essential for professional soccer players and even for players on school or recreational teams. The right exercises help them develop their skills, strengthen their body, and prevent injury. Physical conditioning is one of the most important parts of game preparation. Another important part is fueling the body in the correct way. Learning about the science of nutrition helps soccer players know what foods to eat to give them long-lasting energy and help them build muscle in a healthy way.

Soccer is not an easy sport. Former college soccer coach Ron McEachen has stated, "[Soccer players] do upwards of 200 sprints of varying distances, kick the ball 75 to 100 times, and jump to head the ball as many as 100 times. It's a physical game in which players make full-speed contact with each other as often as 50 times a game."[17] The proper training is important to ensure that players are physically prepared for the toll the sport can take on the body.

Soccer requires both excellent physical fitness and a great deal of technical skill. Players train hard to develop the coordination, muscle strength, endurance, and flexibility that will propel them through a physically challenging match. They also must train smart, using their scientific knowledge to understand both what can be done to improve their performance and the limits of the human body. This allows them to train at a high level while keeping their body safe from injury, which is common in a sport as physically demanding as soccer.

From the Eyes to the Feet

An essential skill in most sports is hand-eye coordination. The eyes constantly receive visual stimuli and send information to the brain about what they see. The brain, in turn, sends signals to the body through the central nervous system—the body's information gathering, processing, and control system—to respond to the visual stimuli. How accurately and quickly the hands reach for, grab, or manipulate an object once the eyes have seen it is a measure of hand-eye coordination. The ability to catch and throw a ball, for example, is second nature for most athletes, and the best can do it without ever looking at their hands—their brain intuitively measures the speed and the direction of an approaching ball and positions their hands perfectly for a catch. This is something soccer goalkeepers, for example, can do with amazing accuracy.

A slightly different skill is also needed in soccer: foot-eye coordination. It works much the same way as hand-eye coordination in that the feet have to respond quickly to what the eyes see. Foot-eye coordination is essential for basic tasks, such as running or climbing stairs—neither of which is easy to do with the eyes closed. The brain needs information from the eyes to direct the movement of the legs and feet. In soccer, foot-eye coordination is fundamental for kicking, dribbling,

ing, dribbling, and trapping a ball. Pelé, who is widely considered one of the best soccer players of all time, has said, "If you ever want to be a decent player, you have to learn to use each foot equally without stopping to think about it."[18]

Soccer training includes drills, such as dribbling through cones or kicking a ball repeatedly against a wall and intercepting it on the rebound, to develop the foot-eye coordination that the world's best soccer players have mastered. Although some level of foot-eye coordination is innate, it takes practice to develop the exceptional level of coordination the best soccer players display on a regular basis. These drills must be repeated over and over again to have an impact on the way the brain processes visual stimuli and the speed with which it sends messages to the feet.

Foot-eye coordination is very important in soccer, so it must be developed through specific drills that are repeated many times.

Think (and Move) Fast!

The brain's coordination of body movement in response to visual stimuli allows soccer players to control the ball. It also guides their balance and reflexes. Balance is an essential soccer skill closely tied to foot-eye coordination. A soccer ball changes direction quickly as it gets passed from player to player. Running at full speed, soccer players keep their eyes on the ball and often must change direction in an instant without losing their balance. Balancing is a complicated process involving the vestibular system in the inner ear that has fluid that shifts as the body moves. The ears send information back to the brain, which combines this information with what the eyes are seeing to signal the muscles to move in a way that restores balance and prevents falling down. Over time and with a lot of practice, soccer players' bodies get used to making abrupt turns in response to the movement of the ball without toppling over at a critical moment in the game.

Another important factor in balancing is proprioception, or kinesthetic awareness. This is the body's sense of where it is in space. Even when soccer players cannot see all their limbs—for example, when focusing on the goal, they cannot constantly look at their feet—they have a sense of how their body is positioned because of proprioception. This "sixth sense" comes from sensors in the body's joints, muscles, and other tissues that send messages to the brain about the position and motion of body parts. These sensors are known as proprioceptors. A strong sense of proprioception is helpful for the development of good balance.

Coordination between the hands, feet, and eyes also relates to reflexes. A reflex is an involuntary, instantaneous response to a stimulus—something heard, seen, or felt. Blinking when an object flies toward one's face is an example of a reflex. A person with slow reflexes may not even flinch or duck if an object were to fly at their face. A person with faster reflexes might have time to duck or put their hands up to deflect the object. An athlete with well-trained reflexes could catch the object. All soccer players must have good reflexes, but reflexes are especially important for goalkeepers. They must be able to respond instantaneously to the ball coming at the goal, putting their hands up to stop it before the other team scores.

It is possible to develop reflexes to respond more quickly to stimuli, especially visual ones. Improving coordination between the eyes, hands, and feet, for example, improves reflexes. Practicing any activity that requires coordination between the hands, feet, and eyes helps athletes develop better reflexes. Soccer drills to improve players' reflexes include having two players face off on the field. One prepares to kick the ball, and the other cannot move until the ball is in motion. The second player then must react quickly to intercept the moving ball. The closer the players stand to one another, the harder this drill will be and the better reflexes it will require. The more time spent practicing such activities, as well as playing actual soccer games, the better a player's reflexes will become. Most professional soccer players have practiced drills such as this one regularly since childhood, so their reflexes are well developed.

Building Muscle Mass

Developing good coordination and reflexes helps soccer players fine-tune their skills, but even before they start to master these important aspects of the game, soccer players must get their bodies in the right physical shape to handle the rigors of a soccer match. They need to be able to kick a soccer ball powerfully, for example. They also must be able to do things such as jog forward and backward, turn, leap to head the soccer ball, and break into a sprint throughout the full 90 minutes of a match without becoming exhausted or losing focus. To carry out these tasks, soccer players focus on two important aspects of fitness: strength and endurance.

Muscles give the body its strength and are the driving force behind any athletic performance. There are three types of muscle tissue: cardiac, smooth, and skeletal. Cardiac muscle tissue is found in the heart, and smooth muscle tissue lines some of

Fighting Through Fatigue

Few soccer players have demonstrated the physical toll the sport can have on the body as dramatically as former soccer superstar Michelle Akers. Her 15-year professional career began in 1985 with the U.S. women's first-ever international match and ended in 2000 due to a long list of physical ailments and injuries. Akers, who scored 105 goals in international matches and helped her team to two World Cup championship titles and an Olympic gold medal, is known as one of the best and toughest women to ever play the sport. On top of being battered with serious physical injuries that ranged from a dislocated shoulder to broken facial bones, Akers was also diagnosed with chronic fatigue syndrome, a long-term condition that results in extreme physical weakness and fatigue. The illness drained her body of the strength to sit up some days and caused severe migraine headaches and stomach problems. Still, Akers continued playing soccer for several years after her diagnosis, despite eventually requiring intravenous fluids after games. Akers left a legacy as one of the most dedicated players—male or female—in the history of the sport.

Michelle Akers managed to play at the highest level of soccer despite her diagnosis of chronic fatigue syndrome because she and her trainers, coaches, and doctors were smart about not pushing her body beyond its limits.

the other internal organs. These types of muscle tissue are not controlled voluntarily. The heart, for example, beats whether a person thinks about it or not. Skeletal muscle tissue, on the other hand, is controlled voluntarily. Skeletal muscles are connected to bones to power the body's movement. They consist of muscle fibers that stretch and relax in a way that is similar to a cluster of rubber bands. Skeletal muscles can be strengthened and made bigger—known as muscular hypertrophy—through exercise.

Developing larger, stronger skeletal muscles is an ongoing process that happens by gently overworking a specific muscle or muscle group until the fibers of muscle tissue become slightly

Exercises specifically meant to strengthen the muscles of the legs are a major part of training and conditioning for soccer players.

damaged. The body quickly repairs the muscle tissue, making it a little hardier in the process to withstand further use. A few days after being overused, the muscle tissue will not only be healed, but it will also be slightly larger and stronger than before. Over time, as an athlete repeatedly breaks down skeletal muscle tissue and allows it to heal, muscles grow in mass and strength.

For soccer players, developing strong leg muscles is important for everything from kicking to maintaining balance during a game. "Players who get knocked off the ball or land on the ground need to improve their footwork and the strength of their hamstrings and quadriceps to enhance their balance," McEachen has said. "The true test is if a player can maintain a good base of support in all situations while competing."[19] Muscular legs not only bring better balance but also more powerful kicks. Large muscles are heavier than small muscles. Since the leg acts like a club during a kick, a heavier leg will swing harder and contact the ball with more force. Strong legs with a good amount of muscle mass are often an advantage for soccer players. During training, a soccer player may concentrate on adding bulk to the lower body using weightlifting techniques to develop the quadriceps on the front of the thigh and the hamstrings along the back of the thigh.

Being too muscular, however, can be a disadvantage in soccer. Precisely because muscle tissue is so heavy, soccer players should not have too much of it weighing down their legs. A soccer game requires a great deal of running. Running on legs that are twice as heavy as every other players' because of their muscle mass could affect another crucial aspect of a soccer player's physical fitness: endurance, or the ability to remain physically active for long periods without tiring.

Think on Your Feet!

An athlete can produce 2 to 3 pints (0.95 to 1.42 L) of sweat per hour during training or a game.

The Importance of Endurance

Superior endurance, probably more than any other physical ability, is the hallmark of soccer. Teams whose players can tolerate intense physical activity from the beginning of a soccer match to the end improve their chances of winning. Teams whose players are exhausted and gasping for air by the end of a match may not fare as well. Just as athletes train their muscles to become bigger and stronger, they also train their entire body to improve endurance. They may begin training by jogging long distances to prepare their body to run the equivalent of several miles every game. However, soccer is not played in a continuous sprint but in repeated bursts of running, broken up by periods of walking, jogging, jumping, and even moving backward. Soccer players must develop endurance, which is also known as stamina, for these demanding activities. One way they do this is by aerobic exercise, which is exercise that is powered by oxygen, such as running for at least 30 minutes.

Although aerobic exercise is important in soccer training, it is not the only kind of exercise required. This is because soccer does not call for the same level of energy to be used at all times. The ability of the muscles to produce bursts of speed even when the body becomes tired is important in soccer. Repeated sprints that raise a person's heart rate beyond the level of typical aerobic exercise are a form of anaerobic exercise—exercise that requires more than the oxygen normally needed by a working muscle, forcing the muscle to break down carbohydrates for energy. This process is called glycolysis, and it creates a byproduct called lactic acid, which builds up in the muscles and makes them feel sore and tired. Every time a muscle is used anaerobically, however, it becomes stronger and better adapted to the activity. Endurance training that demands many short sprints helps a soccer player build muscles that can handle the repeated anaerobic demands of a soccer game.

Soccer players are said to be some of the most physically fit athletes because of their endurance.

"The endurance of a soccer athlete is more than just being able to run forever," soccer coaches Sigi Schmid and Bob Alejo have said. "A high level of endurance will allow the soccer athlete to maintain nearly perfect execution of skills at close to 100 percent effort throughout a match."[20] Consistently using muscles in the right way and pushing slightly and safely beyond what was previously achieved at every practice are how soccer players improve endurance for peak performance during a game.

Fueling the Body

Proper training can only do so much for soccer players. Even the fittest athletes will be limited in their abilities if they do not eat properly and drink enough liquids, because the body depends on having the right types and amounts of nutrients and fluids to work efficiently. An athlete's body requires a constant store of carbohydrates, for example, because living cells convert them into glucose, which is a molecule that releases energy when it is broken apart. Carbohydrates that are not immediately used by cells are stored in the body as glycogen and later converted into glucose as the body's activity levels require. If soccer players do not eat enough carbohydrates to create glycogen reserves in the body before a match, they will run out of glucose before the end, and their starved, fatigued muscles will perform poorly. Even the brain needs glucose for energy to carry out essential soccer tasks such as decision making and maintaining coordination and reflexes, so a player with a poor diet may have a poor mental performance on the field in addition to a poor physical performance.

Some people mistakenly believe athletes require protein more than any other nutrient, but carbohydrates that come from rice, pasta, and fresh vegetables are the mainstay of an athlete's diet. This is especially true of complex carbohydrates, which provide energy for long periods of time. Whole grains, beans, and vegetables are the best sources of complex carbohydrates.

Carbohydrates, not protein, are the primary form of energy used by all parts of the body—from the muscles to the brain. However, protein is still necessary for athletes. It is used in the body for building and repairing muscles. Soccer players try to choose lean sources of protein, or sources without a lot of fat. Fish, chicken, and eggs are common sources of protein for many athletes, including soccer players.

Soccer players also need to drink a lot of water to stay hydrated if they expect to perform at their full potential during a practice or a game. They lose a lot of water through sweat during a match, and water is necessary in the body for many reasons. Having adequate water in the body helps lubricate the joints so they do not stiffen during a game. It also helps muscles contract quickly so that every time a soccer player wants to kick the ball, the muscles respond. Water is needed to bring oxygen to the muscles, and it flushes out some of the lactic acid produced when muscles work anaerobically. Water also helps keep the brain working even when the rest of the body is fatigued. A well-hydrated player feels less tired during a game, pays better attention, and is less likely to feel sore the following day.

Proper hydration is especially important when soccer matches are played outdoors in hot weather. This causes the body to sweat more, so players require more water to replenish what they lost.

Think on Your Feet!

Anaerobic exercise involves pushing the body to as much as 85 percent of its maximum heart rate.

The physical effects of dehydration, or lack of sufficient water in the body, can be devastating. Sports nutrition expert Don MacLaren stated, "A mild degree of dehydration will impair skilled performance and affect strength, stamina, and speed. An adequate fluid intake is necessary to offset the effects of dehydration."[21] Soccer players drink water throughout the day so they are well hydrated long before they begin to exercise and sweat heavily. It is also important for them to drink throughout a practice or a game. Athletic conditioning, muscle strength, and hours of practicing skills mean nothing to a soccer player if their body lacks essential fuel and fluids.

Staying Flexible

A well-fed, well-hydrated soccer player builds muscle more efficiently and has more endurance than one who is dehydrated or undernourished, and this also lowers the risk of getting sore or injured during a practice or a game. However, even the fittest and best-nourished soccer players may develop stiff muscles and be more likely to sustain an injury if they focus only on strength and endurance training and ignore flexibility, or the ability of muscle tissue to stretch for a greater range of motion. This is a key component of physical fitness and one that good soccer players spend time developing.

All skeletal muscles work by stretching and contracting, and like a rubber band, the more often they are stretched, the more pliable they become. Muscles that are not stretched regularly may remain constantly contracted. Since muscles create all their power by

Practicing Plyometrics

Many different exercises have been used by soccer players throughout the sport's history. As understanding of the human body and its development has improved, so has the effectiveness of training methods. In recent years, a type of training called plyometrics has become popular because of its success. Plyometrics involves explosive exercises that quickly stretch and contract muscles, exerting maximum force in short intervals of time. Stretching makes muscles longer, and contracting shortens them. Doing exercises that stretch and contract muscles increases muscle power and speed. Jumping is a common plyometric exercise, and soccer players use different kinds of jumps from different positions in their plyometric training.

contracting, or flexing, to move a bone, a muscle that is already contracted cannot flex any more to help the leg swing into a kick, for example. This can happen in muscles that are overdeveloped through too much exercise. People who have this problem are said to be "muscle bound," and this problem weakens a muscle, even if it is large and well developed from strength training.

Stretching is a part of all athletic training because it boosts performance and decreases the risk of injury.

Stretching exercises improve muscle flexibility, enhancing a muscle's ability to contract. Many stretching exercises involve holding the body in a specific position to lengthen the muscles. Flexibility is one of the most important aspects of training for soccer players. Not only does it improve their playing, but it is also critical for preventing sports injuries, something about which soccer players must always be careful. No matter how hard soccer players practice improving their coordination and reflexes or how physically fit they become, an injury could bring a talented player's career to an end. Therefore, soccer players must educate themselves about the causes of common soccer injuries so they can train and play in a way that minimizes their chances of hurting themselves while still allowing them to give their maximum effort on the pitch.

Chapter 5

The Impact of Injuries

Soccer is a physically demanding sport that pushes an athlete's body to its limits and, in some cases, beyond them. There is always a risk of injury in sports—whether from overuse of certain body parts, contact with other players, improper conditioning, or even accidents and seemingly random occurrences. For example, in 2010, the international soccer superstar David Beckham tore his Achilles tendon—the tissue that connects the calf to the heel—during a routine moment in a match. Beckham returned to the sport after a period of rest and rehabilitation, but such a major injury sustained by one of the sport's brightest stars called attention to the risks soccer players take when they play the sport they love.

Soccer is considered a contact sport, which means that players often hit each other or an object (in this case, the soccer ball) with some amount of force. Although there is certainly a risk of injury due to contact in these sports, it is not as high as in many collision sports, such as American football, which are sports that feature athletes purposely hitting each other or objects with great force.

Injury prevention and treatment is an important part of understanding the sport of soccer. Dislocated joints, broken bones, pulled or torn muscles, and concussions are just some of the most common injuries soccer players suffer on the pitch or in practice. Knowing what causes these injuries, what can be done to prevent them, and what methods are used to treat them most effectively can help players stay as safe as possible and even prolong their career.

David Beckham returned to the pitch six months after tearing his Achilles tendon.

Ankle Injuries

Injuries to the lower body, such as the one suffered by Beckham, are the most common soccer injuries, and there is one particular body part that is most at risk: the ankle. Soccer players perform many sprints and sudden turns and have frequent contact with the feet and legs of other players, all of which can put unnatural force on the ankles. The ankle joint consists of four bones: the tibia and the fibula, the long bones that form the shin; the talus, a small bone that creates a ball-and-socket joint by fitting into the socket where the bases of the fibula and tibia meet; and the calcaneus, or heel bone, which supports the talus. All four bones are held together by ligaments—tough, elastic-like bands that attach bones to each other at joints. There are four major ligaments in the ankle. Three are on the lateral side, facing away from the opposite ankle, and one is on the medial side (sometimes called the deltoid ligament), facing the opposite ankle. The ankle is a strong joint, designed to hold up throughout a lifetime of walking, running, and jumping, but it is not immune to severe damage, such as the major twisting that can happen during a soccer game.

If the ankle twists hard enough, the ligaments will stretch beyond their natural range of motion and may tear, either slightly or completely. Damage caused by the wrenching of ligaments is called a sprain, a serious injury that can take weeks or months to heal. Ankle sprains are some of the most common soccer injuries.

Sometimes, the wrenching or twisting motion is powerful enough to dislocate a joint, or pull the ball portion of one bone out of the socket portion of another. Because ankles are such sturdy joints, a dislocated ankle rarely happens unless an impact or collision breaks a shinbone. A dislocated joint often causes ligament damage and can cut off the blood supply to the affected area. Dislocations are serious injuries that require emergency medical treatment.

Tough on the Knees

Ankles are not the only joints that can be sprained or dislocated. Knees are another common site of injury in soccer players. The knee is a hinge joint, or a joint that moves only back and forth. It connects the femur bone of the thigh to the tibia, the thicker of the shin's two parallel bones. The patella, a small bone often called the kneecap, is part of this joint as well. There is a pad of cartilage between the femur and the tibia called the meniscus, which acts as a cushion between the leg bones.

Several important ligaments connect the parts of the knee. The collateral ligaments run along the inner and outer sides of the joint and prevent the tibia from swinging side to side instead of front to back. Two cruciate ligaments, so named because they cross each other to form an X ("cruciate" means "cross shaped"), prevent the knee joint from rotating or twisting too much. One of these ligaments, the anterior cruciate ligament (ACL), keeps the knee from hyperextending, or moving beyond its natural range of motion. The other, the posterior cruciate ligament (PCL), keeps the tibia from moving too far backward.

Sprained or torn knee ligaments happen often in soccer. A tear to the ACL happens when the knee is forced to twist unnaturally. This is a common and serious soccer injury. An ACL can be torn

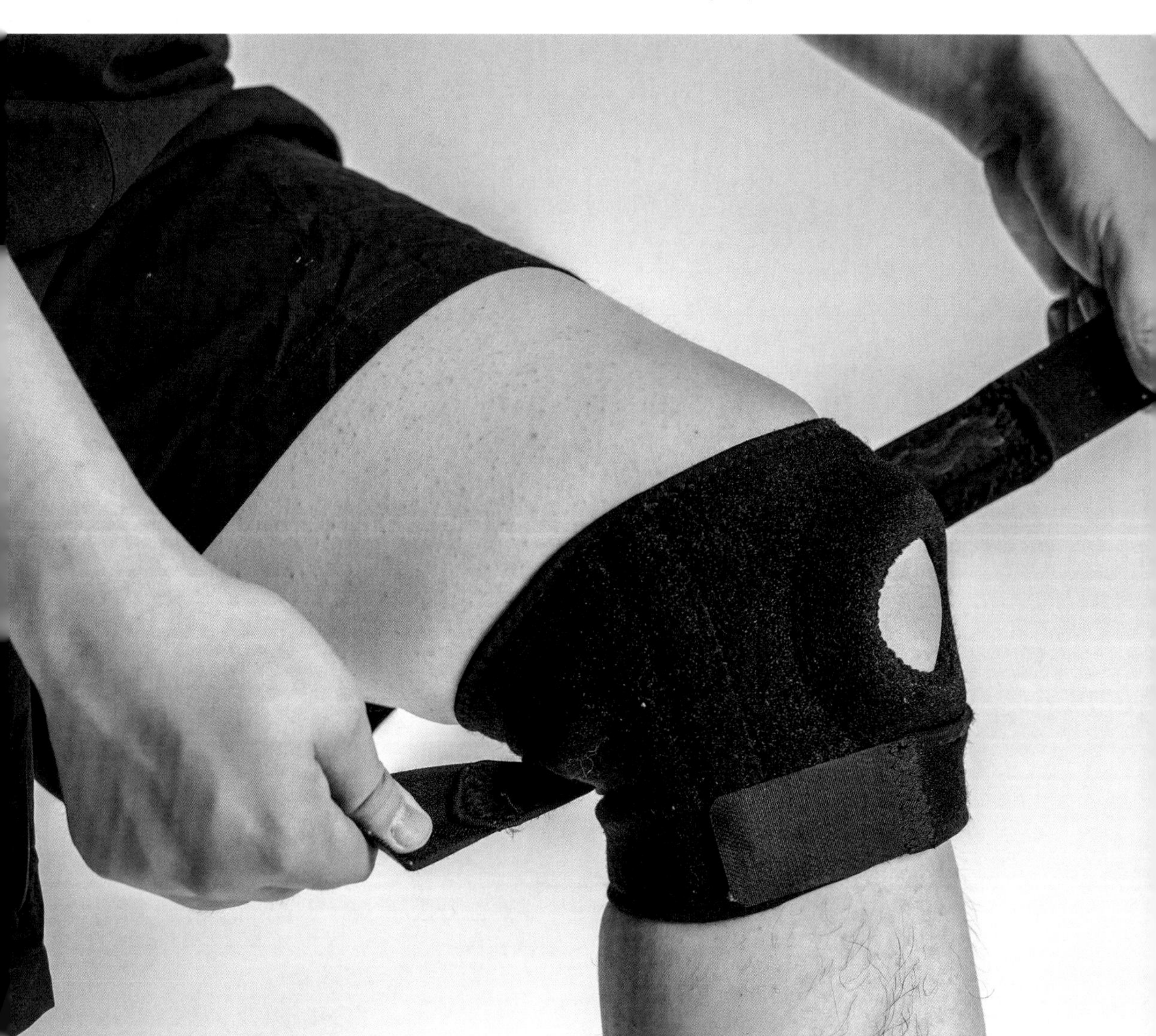

Many soccer players wear knee braces to stabilize the joint after an injury.

if a sprinting player suddenly stops running to change direction or if a player's lower leg is held down by another player during an attempted turn. A torn knee ligament such as the ACL usually requires surgery and months of physical therapy—a kind of supervised exercise program that targets an injured body part to rebuild mobility and strength. Many soccer players return to the game once a torn ligament is healed, but previously damaged joints tend to be weaker, more painful, and prone to repeat injuries. "Because of the unusual stresses placed on knees in soccer," Richard Witzig has stated, "serious knee injuries are the most common physical injury to force retirement. Indeed, more than 30% of former players will experience chronic pain … on retirement."[22]

Think on Your Feet!

Female soccer players have a higher risk of tearing their ACL than male soccer players.

Muscle and Tendon Injuries

Unlike ligaments, which cannot be strengthened to handle more stress, muscles can be made stronger. However, muscles can still be a site of serious injury for soccer players. They are especially vulnerable when a player's body is tired. Overexertion, or doing more physical activity than the body can handle, sometimes results in muscle damage. Colliding with another player can also harm muscles. Such situations can tear a muscle's fibrous tissue. In soccer, the most common site for muscle tears, sometimes referred to as pulled or strained muscles, are the hamstrings, which are groups of muscles that run along the back of the thighs.

There are three levels, or grades, of muscle tears. A grade 1 tear involves less than 5 percent of the muscle but causes pain and stiffness. Needing two to three weeks to heal, a grade 1 muscle tear usually causes no additional problems, but if the player does not rest the muscle, the pain often does not get better. A grade 2 muscle tear involves breakage across much of the muscle's tissue but stops short of tearing the muscle completely in two. A player who suffers a second-degree tear usually cannot contract the muscle at all without severe pain. This kind of tear often involves swelling. A grade 3 muscle tear is a rupture, which is a complete tear that separates the muscle in two. The muscle is then completely unable to contract, and the player cannot move the affected limb normally. The torn ends of the ruptured muscle may ball up to form large lumps under the skin, and sometimes a gap can be felt under the skin where the muscle separated. This injury also causes internal bleeding at the site of the rupture. Ruptured muscles sometimes require surgery to join the pieces of muscle back together. Even after the

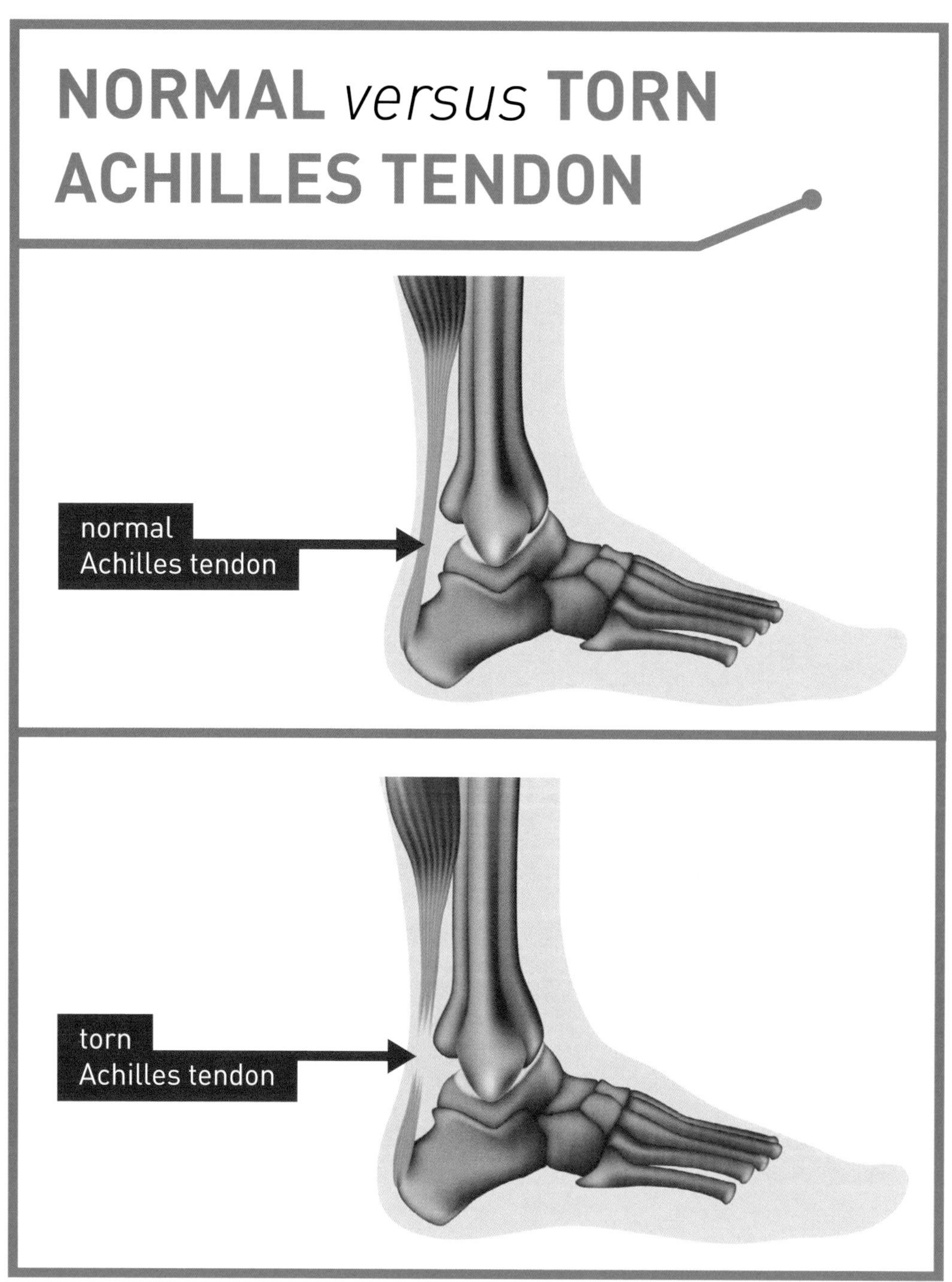

A torn Achilles tendon is a devastating injury for a soccer player, but with proper treatment, it does not necessarily have to end their career.

muscle heals, scar tissue remains. This weakens and stiffens the muscle and makes it vulnerable to future injuries.

Just as muscles cannot work properly when badly torn, a muscle will be useless if its tendon, the band of fibrous tissue that connects it to a bone, is damaged. One of the most important tendons for soccer players is the Achilles tendon. The Achilles tendon is essential for walking, running, and jumping, but the force put on this tendon during an aggressive soccer game is sometimes too much. If the tendon tears, either partly or completely, then the calf muscle will be unable to contract normally. Without its anchor to the heel, the muscle may ball up in the back of the leg. The player will be unable to run or even walk. When David Beckham tore his Achilles tendon in 2010, his coach described what happened to his muscle: "He felt the muscle begin to come up, which is a typical symptom when you break an Achilles tendon."[23]

An injured Achilles tendon often requires surgery and can have serious consequences for soccer players. It takes a long time to come back from such a severe injury, and the rehabilitation process involves months of physical therapy to regain strength and range of motion.

Think on Your Feet!

ACL injuries make soccer players miss more playing time than any other injury.

Fracture Facts

Injuries to ligaments, muscles, and tendons can have major consequences for soccer players, but the bones to which the muscles, ligaments, and tendons attach, especially in the lower leg, are also put into many risky situations during a game. High-speed, high-force kicks and tackles in soccer often pit one player's feet and shins against another's, causing a clash of bones. Bones are strong, but they can be damaged by a forceful blow, such as a high-speed collision between soccer players. A crack or break in a bone's surface is called a fracture.

Bones consist of a dense outer covering called compact bone, which surrounds a core of spongy bone (also known as cancellous bone), and bone marrow, where blood cells are produced. A fracture in a bone's surface is a serious injury that usually causes severe pain and swelling in the tissues surrounding the bone. Most bone fractures require medical treatment, which includes repositioning the broken bone and encasing the limb in a cast for several weeks to give the bone time to heal. Some bone fractures are worse than others. The best-case scenario for a broken bone is a closed or simple fracture—a crack in the bone that does not cause part of the bone to shift and damage surrounding tissue and break the skin. A worse kind of break is a compound or open fracture, in which the bone on either side of the fracture spears into surrounding tissue or even pierces through the skin. Compound fractures can cause serious bleeding and tissue damage as well as excruciating pain. They require surgery and the use of plates, screws, and wires to realign the bones properly. A third type of fracture is a comminuted fracture, or a fracture in which the bone shatters into pieces. This kind of fracture may also require surgery and a long period of recovery during which the bone must be kept immobile in a cast in order to heal.

At the college level and in professional leagues, where soccer players move fast and are very physical and competitive, bone injuries are more common. Because severely broken bones are some of the most shocking and memorable injuries that occur on a soccer field, they receive a lot of attention from spectators, coaches, referees, and players. After a particularly bad incident, the player who caused a collision is sometimes accused of foul play. However, in a game as fast-paced as soccer, players know collisions hard enough to break bones are bound to happen.

A Career in Physical Therapy

Physical therapists are health care professionals who develop individualized plans of treatment for patients who cannot move and function normally because of an injury or other medical condition. Physical therapists help athletes recover after a severe injury, such as a broken bone or a torn muscle, ligament, or tendon. They create a plan for each patient to reduce pain, restore range of motion, and keep muscles strong and flexible while the patient is recovering. Physical therapists help injured athletes return to competition as quickly as possible. They need a master's or doctorate degree in physical therapy and must pass their state's required examinations in order to obtain a license to practice. They are employed by hospitals, clinics, or private practices and often work evenings and weekends to fit their patients' schedules. In addition to a strong background in science, including physics, biology, and anatomy, they must have good interpersonal skills and empathy when working with athletes, who often need special encouragement and may fear their career in their sport is over after a severe injury.

A physical therapist is often an important part of an athlete's support system as they recover from a major injury.

Although serious injuries such as broken bones are not as common among youth soccer players, there has been a dramatic rise in such injuries among children in recent years. Serious injuries among youth soccer players—excluding head injuries—increased by 60 percent between 2004 and 2014. Experts believe the increased physical play on the pitch is responsible for this dramatic rise in injuries. Brian Hafter, a coach and referee in girls' soccer leagues in California, stated, "There's no question that nowadays the players are much more physical, challenging for the ball, and as a result, can put themselves and their opponents in situations that can lead to more serious injuries."[24]

Concussions in Soccer

Many soccer injuries happen below the waist, but the head can also be at risk. Soccer is a unique sport in that players typically wear no helmet or other protective headgear, yet they frequently strike their head against the ball to stop its progress, move it up the field, or try to score a goal. Some sports medicine experts suspect that repeatedly heading the ball might cause many small head injuries that accumulate to cause brain damage in some players, which is similar to the way professional boxers sometimes suffer brain damage from taking repeated blows to the head and face. A study published in February 2017 revealed that repeatedly heading the ball—something soccer players do often in practice—increases a soccer player's risk of developing concussion symptoms.

A concussion is a serious brain injury that happens when the head is hit or jolted in a way that causes it to move back and forth too rapidly. This causes the brain to move around in the skull in a dangerous way. Only 7 percent of soccer injuries suffered by children ages 7 to 17 are concussions, but they are among the most serious injuries that can occur during a match or practice. Severe concussions in soccer are more often a result of hitting another player, a goal post, or the ground than heading the ball. Sometimes, soccer players dive or fall to the ground, and their head is suddenly on the same level as other players' kicking feet. Goalkeepers often find themselves in such a position as they lunge for the ball to keep the other team from scoring. Even more than a broken bone or a tear to a muscle, tendon, or ligament, a head injury can remove a player from the game of soccer permanently.

An extensive amount of research has been done in recent years on concussions and their long-term effects on a person's health. This has led to a sharp increase in awareness of the danger of brain injuries and the importance of evaluating athletes who have experienced a hit to the head for concussion symptoms, which include dizziness, blurry vision, and nausea. Although

In 2015, professional soccer player Ali Krieger suffered a serious head injury during a match. When she returned to the pitch later that season, she wore headgear designed to protect her by absorbing some of the force from any hit to the head.

Mental Health Matters

The mental health of athletes is as important as their physical health. Elite athletes, such as those playing soccer in college or professionally, are often under a lot of stress and place a lot of pressure on themselves to succeed. Athletes who are trying to come back from an injury or who have experienced a period of poor play known as a slump deal with additional stressors. It is helpful for athletes to prioritize their mental health the same way they take care of their physical health, so it is not unusual for athletes to see sports psychologists to help them deal with the pressure of competing at a high level.

Sports psychologists are professionals who help athletes cope with the psychological and emotional stresses that can affect how they perform. A sports psychologist may work with an athlete to develop healthy attitudes toward games and matches, decrease their performance anxiety, increase their self-esteem, and help them cope with an injury or difficult loss on a big stage. Sports psychologists need at least a master's degree in psychology, paired with knowledge of sports science and experience working with athletes. Sports psychologists may work for a professional sports team; for a high school, college, or university; or in private practice.

it may seem frightening to see that the rate of head injuries among youth soccer players increased by nearly 1,600 percent from 1990 to 2014, experts believe that dramatic increase is due in part to more people reporting and treating concussions in the correct way. Dr. Andrew Gregory, a professor at Vanderbilt University Medical Center stated, "[The] concussion rate [is] going up … across the board … because [of] increased recognition … There are state laws [that say] if you have concussions you have to be seen. Parents, physicians, coaches, and players are more aware of it."[25] This increased awareness will hopefully lead to increased safety measures—not just in soccer, but in all sports.

Safety First!

Despite the risks soccer poses to the head and the rest of the body, players equip themselves with very little protective gear. Compared to sports such as American football and hockey, in which nearly every inch of a player's body is protected, a soccer player's protection mainly comes from shin guards worn under their socks

Shin guards are the only required piece of protective gear for soccer players.

to minimize pain and injury to these sensitive spots caused by getting kicked or hit by the ball. Soccer players can also wear other protective gear if they want to, as long as it does not endanger other players or provide a distinct competitive advantage. Some soccer players choose to wear a mouth guard to protect their teeth and gums, and some wear special padded shorts to help protect their legs or headgear to protect their head.

Safety is an area of athletics that can always be improved. As people learn more about what causes common soccer injuries, that knowledge is put to use to make it safer for those who play the sport. Technological advancements such as protective headgear are paving the way for a safer future for the sport of soccer. In addition, other technological advancements are impacting the sport's future in different—but no less impressive—ways.

Chapter 6

Technology in Soccer

Soccer is generally the same sport that was played in English schools in the 1800s. Part of what remains so appealing about it is that it is a relatively simple game, requiring only a ball and two goals. However, that does not mean the sport is stuck in the past. It is constantly evolving as new technological advancements are introduced, making equipment safer, making training more effective, and pushing the sport into the future.

From robot kickers to feet-powered fields, some of the latest soccer technology seems straight out of a futuristic movie or comic book. However, these developments are not the stuff of science fiction; they are the result of scientific facts being put into practice in new and creative ways.

Building a Better Ball

Although the basic design of a soccer ball has remained largely unchanged for more than a century, some important technological developments have been made to create the best possible ball, especially for major events such as the World Cup. Improvements in how soccer balls are tested and analyzed have led to the creation of a more aerodynamic shape.

Before the 2014 World Cup, the Brazuca soccer ball was put through many different tests to study its aerodynamics. Scientists in Japan tested the ball in a wind tunnel, which is a chamber in which air is blown at a known velocity past an object to study its aerodynamics. Wind tunnels are best known for testing aircraft, but they can also be used to test much smaller objects, such as soccer balls.

Scientists discovered that a smoother ball is actually a less ideal design than a ball that has small bumps or dimples on its surface. A smoother ball creates more drag, or air resistance, around it, which causes it to behave more unpredictably in the air. The ball used in the previous World Cup—the Jabulani— was relatively smooth, which made it difficult for goalkeepers to stop because of its unpredictable movement. Knowing this, the designers of the Brazuca created a ball that is covered with small bumps to decrease the drag around the ball.

The motion of the air around the Brazuca is difficult to see with the naked eye because air is invisible. However, scientists at the National Aeronautics and Space Administration (NASA) used lasers and smoke to show the movement of the air around a Brazuca ball in a wind tunnel in a way that can be easily seen. Scientists pumped smoke into the tunnel in a controlled fashion and used lasers to highlight the movement of the smoke at different speeds. The ball was also tested in a water channel that used dye that appears under a black light to show the movement of fluid around it.

The testing of the Brazuca was seen by employees at NASA as a fun way to get people interested in aerodynamics. As Rabi Mehta, chief of the Experimental Aero-Physics Branch at NASA's Ames Research Center in Moffett Field, California, said, "Sports provide a great opportunity to introduce the next generation of researchers to our field of aerodynamics by showing them something they can relate to."[26]

The Brazuca was tested in another creative way by Japanese scientists. They built a robot kicker to test the Brazuca as well as the Jabulani. The robot kicked

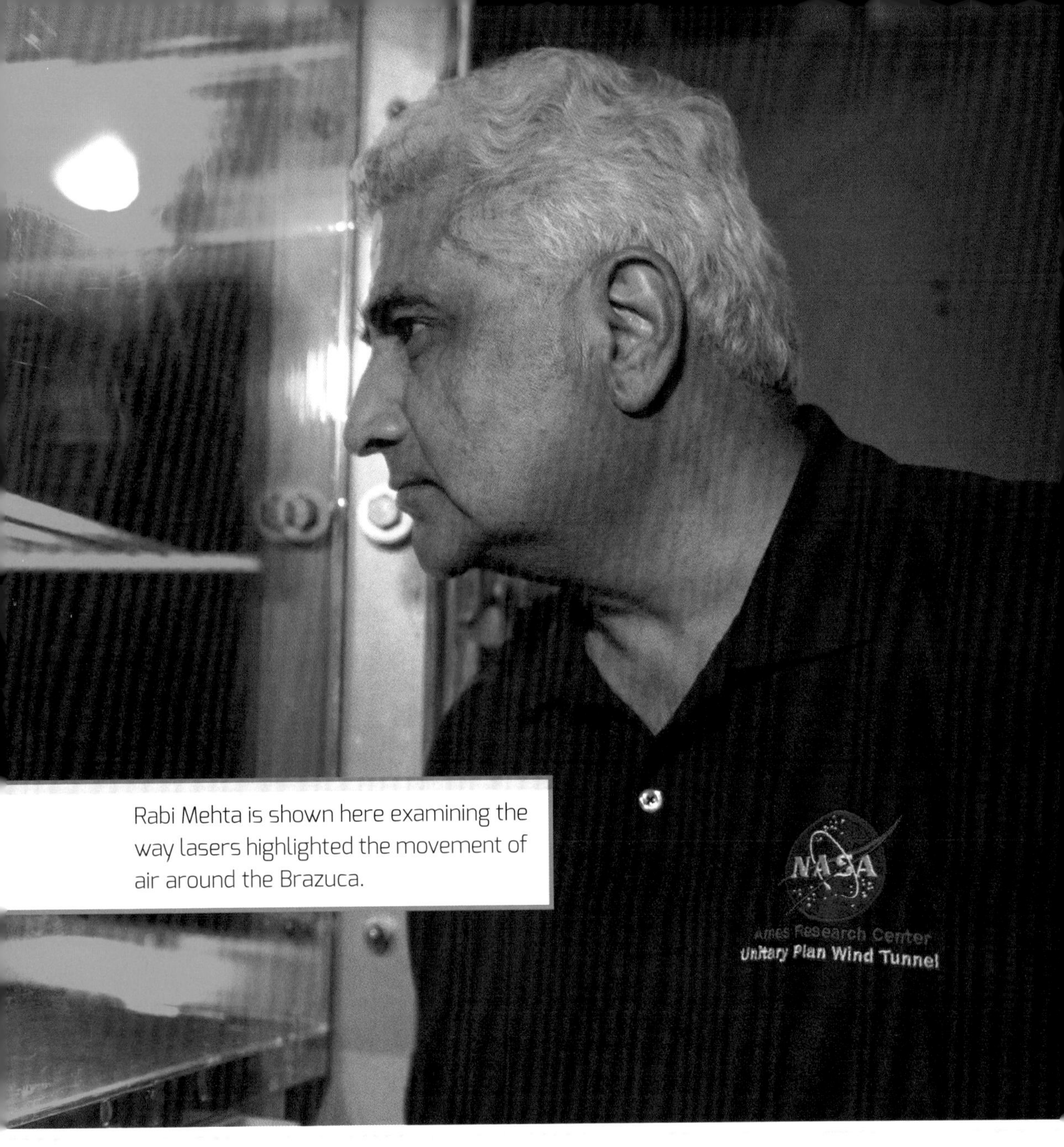

Rabi Mehta is shown here examining the way lasers highlighted the movement of air around the Brazuca.

each ball many times, with the scientists changing its positioning so different parts of its robotic foot connected with the ball. They found that the Brazuca's path was much more predictable and the Brazuca was much more likely to hit its target than the Jabulani—no matter which part of a player's foot hit the ball. These tests were more reliable than human testing because the researchers could completely control the robot kicker, ensuring more accurate results.

RoboCup

Robots are not used only to test soccer balls; they also play soccer on teams and in leagues. In 1997, the first official Robot World Cup—commonly known as RoboCup—conference and games were held. RoboCup is an initiative designed to promote interest in and awareness of robotics and artificial intelligence (AI) systems. It aims to do this by offering the public a relatable and entertaining platform to view robotic achievements as scientists and engineers work toward a particular goal. That goal, as stated by RoboCup officials, is that "[b]y the middle of the 21st century, a team of fully autonomous humanoid robot soccer players shall win a soccer game, complying with the official rules of FIFA, against the winner of the most recent World Cup."[1] RoboCup developers believe such a goal is attainable because it only took 50 years for the invention of the airplane to develop into the space program and for the creation of the first digital computer to lead to the first computer to beat a human at chess.

Although no robot team is ready yet to take on their human counterparts in a soccer match, RoboCup events held between robot teams take place around the world every year. These events are attended by passionate fans of both soccer and robotics.

1. "Objective," RoboCup, 2016. www.robocup.org/objective.

RoboCup events promote the field of robotics in a fun and memorable way.

If the Shoe Fits

Two of the most important aspects of soccer are the ball and the feet used to kick it. Therefore, it makes sense that the shoes soccer players wear, also known as cleats or boots, should go through the same kind of serious testing that balls such as the Brazuca have gone through. One company in particular has taken footwear testing to the next level. Nike is one of the leaders in athletic footwear, and it has taken great care in recent years to make sure that its soccer shoes are the best they can be. To do this, they have used the latest technology to design and test their shoes, most notably the Magista 2.

The Magista 2 was designed with the help of a system called Finite Element Analysis (FEA). This is a computer system that aims to accurately predict how a product, such as a soccer boot, will react in the real world. By using the FEA system, designers at Nike were able to figure out the best placement of studs on the bottom of the shoes to create the ideal amount of friction on any surface in any weather.

The different patterns of studs were quickly created using a 3D printer. This process was seen as a game-changer for athletic shoe development. Now, a new design could be printed in hours, where before the development of 3D printing technology, it would have taken weeks or months. As Nathan VanHook, a senior design director at Nike Football, said, "You see things right away … We can take the lever and say, 'Let's see what the most extreme [thing to do] is,' and are able to prototype and iterate superfast."[27]

The amount of research that went into the creation of the Magista 2 can even be seen in the color patterns on the shoe itself. Areas of the foot that are most likely to come into contact with the ball are highlighted with red. These areas were discovered through long periods of testing using motion capture technology. With more than 20 cameras and an advanced 3D system, Nike's lab captured the movements of athletes kicking and controlling a soccer ball. Designers then used the footage the cameras captured to model how the foot and ball interact in different situations.

As soccer players become more finely-tuned athletic machines, their gear has to match their skills. Nike and other athletic apparel companies are leading the way in the quest to make soccer players' clothing and shoes work for them instead of creating a barrier between them and the next level of success in their sport.

Think on Your Feet!

Nike's research is conducted in its Sport Research Lab, which is a secret facility in Oregon that requires a screening process before someone can be granted access—even for other Nike employees.

A Turf War

The 2015 Women's World Cup was played in Canada on artificial turf. This became a major news story because this event was the first FIFA World Cup—for men or women—to be played on a surface other than natural grass. Arguments were made in the lead-up to and in the aftermath of the tournament both for and against the use of artificial turf on the game's biggest stage.

Artificial turf is a synthetic, or man-made, surface designed to look, feel, and behave like real grass. Those in favor of its use believe it saves money because it does not require watering, fertilizing, or care such as cutting. Artificial turf also allows games to be played even in the rain, which would damage natural grass. Although there are many people, including many FIFA officials, who support the use of artificial turf, a large number of soccer players have spoken out against its use. They have stated that it is difficult to predict how a ball will bounce on turf, and they have complained about the heat on the field, which has been known to melt players' cleats.

Before the 2015 World Cup, women's soccer players, such as U.S. star Sydney Leroux, voiced their concerns about playing on artificial turf. Leroux was especially concerned about the "turf burns" players sustain when they slide on artificial turf:

It's really sad women have to be guinea pigs for this. Once every four years it is a dream to play in the World Cup. And to have to think, OK, we have the potential for seven games at the World Cup. The first couple games, I have to be careful and take care of my body because you saw my leg [which was covered in turf burns]. How am I supposed to play after that with the same aggressiveness? I can't come out completely bandaged up. We will have to figure out a way that when sliding, we can continue to play without chewing up our body. The issue is: How are you supposed to play with the legs that I had? And I'm sure it would be even worse in a World Cup, where you're giving everything and more.[28]

The turf burns sustained by soccer players are concerning for reasons beyond the pain that comes with them. Many players, parents of young players, and coaches have become increasingly worried about the cancer risk posed by playing on artificial turf fields. Former player and coach Amy Griffin compiled a list of athletes who have been diagnosed with cancer after playing on artificial turf, and, as of January 2017, 237 athletes are on her list. One prevailing theory about the link between artificial soccer turf and cancer is that the rubber pellets—often pieces of old tires—used as filler can get into turf-burn cuts and cause cancer. More scientific studies need to be conducted to determine whether there is a definitive link between artificial turf and cancer. Until then, the debate about using the latest turf technology rages on.

The fight between female soccer players and FIFA over the playing surface in the 2015 World Cup was known as the "turf war," and it resulted in a gender discrimination lawsuit, which was eventually dropped when it became clear that FIFA was not going to budge on its use of artificial turf.

Measuring Muscle Movement

Soccer players use many muscles and nerves, but it has been difficult to determine exactly which muscles are used during any particular movement. However, scientists are now using electromyography (EMG) to see exactly which muscles and nerves are used during specific activities, such as kicking a ball. EMG is a procedure in which electrodes are placed on the skin and transmit information to a computer about the use of specific muscles and nerves. EMG can be used to diagnose problems with muscles and nerves, or it can be used by researchers to see exactly what body parts are involved in specific activities. In soccer, knowing which muscles and nerves are used in different movements helps prevent overuse and can be used to see if exercises are training the right body parts.

Goal-Line Technology

The playing surface is not the only place on the pitch where technology has changed how the game is played. The line that determines whether or not a player has scored a goal has also been impacted by technological developments. The latest goal-line technology is being used by FIFA to determine whether or not a ball has crossed over the line, resulting in a goal.

One advancement in goal-line technology is the use of cameras and computer software to determine whether a goal has been scored. As many as seven cameras capture the movement of the ball to give an accurate picture of whether or not it has completely crossed the line. Another system used by FIFA involves magnetic fields generated by cables placed under the ground and around the goal. Receptors are then placed in the ball, and these receptors interact with the magnetic field to give computers information about the ball's placement in and around the goal.

Once the computer systems have analyzed the ball's position, a message is sent to the match officials as quickly as possible, generally within one second. The message states whether or not the play resulted in a goal, and it pops up on a watch worn by the officials. This futuristic technology aims to keep the game fast and fair.

Think on Your Feet!

FIFA began using goal-line technology in tournaments in 2012.

Shown here is a machine used to create a magnetic field around a soccer goal in Germany to help officials determine whether or not a goal was scored.

Technology in Training

Training is another aspect of soccer that has been influenced by major technological advances. Wearable heart rate monitors have become common sights on average people—not just athletes—in recent years. However, soccer trainers and coaches have been using them for more than a decade. Although that technology is still an important part of training for professional and college soccer players, it has been combined with another technological development to produce even more personalized training programs. As Dawn Scott, the strength and fitness coach for the U.S. Women's National Team (USWNT) explained,

> *Heart rate monitoring has been around for over 10 years now, but in the past five years there has been an increase in the use of GPS technology in soccer and sports generally, which is basically like a car's satellite navigation tracking every single movement and impact a player makes on the field.*[29]

Wearable monitors record a player's heart rate and GPS and transmit that information back to trainers and coaches. This data is then used to determine the best training regimen and workload for each player. The GPS technology measures how much ground a player covers while running during practice, while the heart rate monitor measures how hard their body is working as they cover that ground. These two measurements are used together to indicate a player's overall level of fitness and to help coaches and trainers get them into game shape. As Scott said,

> *By combining the heart rate and GPS, firstly it allows you to determine how players cope with a certain workload and gives a good indication of the fitness level for players. If two players have the same external load from the GPS, but one player's heart rate is higher, it suggests that their endurance system is not as well developed … Once you know the positional load you can then use that as a gauge and indication of your physical load during training, as well as ensure players are prepared for the load they will experience during a game.*[30]

Analyzing the GPS and heart rate data from the wearable monitors allows trainers and coaches to work with players to get them in their best shape without pushing them too hard. It helps prevent injuries and ensures that players receive a manageable amount of playing time during a game, which can lead to more success on the pitch.

A Bright Future

Soccer players run up and down the pitch for 90 minutes every game. That is a lot of kinetic energy, and two soccer fields an ocean apart have found a way to use that kinetic energy to their benefit.

This neighborhood pitch in Brazil uses the kinetic energy from the feet of soccer players to power the lights around it.

In 2014, a soccer field was opened in Brazil that used the kinetic energy from players' feet to power the lights around the field. A similar field opened in Nigeria in 2016.

These fields use tiles to collect the kinetic energy from the movement of players' feet, turning it into electricity that is stored until it is needed to power the floodlights that illuminate the fields after dark. Both fields also use solar panels to collect additional energy from the sun, which is used with the kinetic energy from the players to provide enough power to turn on the lights.

This creative use of renewable energy sources is important for developing countries, where electricity is still not available to everyone. The lighted fields are meant to be a safe place for people to play the sport they love after dark.

This kind of technology is being used to help soccer remain a universal sport for many years to come. With scientific ideas such as this one being put into practice around the world, the future of soccer looks bright.

Notes

Chapter 1: Soccer Through the Centuries

1. Quoted in David Goldblatt, *The Ball Is Round: A Global History of Soccer*. New York, NY: Riverhead Books, 2006, p. 3.
2. Nigel B. Crowther, *Sport in Ancient Times*. Westport, CT: Praeger, 2007, p. 4.
3. Goldblatt, *The Ball Is Round*, p. 12.
4. Richard Witzig. *The Global Art of Soccer*. New Orleans, LA: Cusiboy Publishing, 2006, p. 9.
5. Quoted in Jean Fievet, "Will World Cup 2010 Be Most-Watched TV Event?," ABC News, June 11, 2010. abcnews.go.com/International/Media/world-cup-mania-kicks-off-world/story?id=10884963.
6. Witzig, *The Global Art of Soccer*, p. 7.

Chapter 2: Physics on the Pitch

7. John Wesson, *The Science of Soccer*. New York, NY: CRC Press, 2002, p. 72.
8. Seyed Hamid Hamraz and Seyed Shams Feyzabadi, "General Purpose Learning Machine Using K-Nearest Neighbors Algorithm." In *Robot Soccer World Cup IX*, edited by Ansgar Bredenfeld, Adam Jacoff, Itsuki Noda, and Yasutake Takahashi. Berlin, Germany: Springer-Verlag, 2006, p. 532.
9. Wesson, *The Science of Soccer*, p. 81.
10. Jim Puhalla, Jeff Krans, and Mike Goatley, *Sports Fields: A Manual for Design Construction and Maintenance*. Hoboken, NJ: John Wiley & Sons, 1999, p. 278.

Chapter 3: The Mechanics of Movement

11. Nate Scott, "Carli Lloyd Put on the Greatest World Cup Final Performance Ever," *USA Today*, July 6, 2015. ftw.usatoday.com/2015/07/carli-lloyd-put-on-the-greatest-world-cup-final-performance-ever.

12. Cameron Bauer, *Algebra for Athletes*, 2nd ed. New York, NY: Nova Science Publishers Inc., 2007, p. 96.
13. Gene Klein, "Corner Kicks and Throw-Ins." In *Attacking Soccer: Tactics and Drills for High-Scoring Offense*, edited by Joseph A. Luxbacher. Champaign, IL: Human Kinetics, 1999, p. 107.
14. Klein, "Corner Kicks and Throw-Ins," p. 107.
15. Peter Mellor and Tony Waiters, "Goalkeeping Excellence." In *The Soccer Coaching Bible*, edited by the National Soccer Coaches Association of America. Champaign, IL: Human Kinetics Publishers, Inc., 2004, p. 164.

Chapter 4: Training to Be the Best

16. Witzig, *The Global Art of Soccer*, p. 25.
17. Ron McEachen, "Training for High-Level Soccer Fitness." In *The Soccer Coaching Bible*, edited by the National Soccer Coaches Association of America. Champaign, IL: Human Kinetics Publishers, Inc., 2004, p. 116.
18. Quoted in Gavin Mortimer, *A History of Football in 100 Objects*. London, UK: Serpent's Tail, 2012.
19. McEachen.,"Training for High-Level Soccer Fitness," p. 118.
20. Sigi Schmid and Bob Alejo, *Complete Conditioning for Soccer*. Champaign, IL: Human Kinetics Publishers, Inc., 2002, p. 3.
21. Don MacLaren, "Nutrition." *In Science and Soccer*, 2nd ed., edited by Thomas Reilly and A. Mark Williams. New York, NY: Routledge, 2005, p. 73.

Chapter 5: The Impact of Injuries

22. Witzig, *The Global Art of Soccer*, p. 108.
23. Quoted in Andrew Das, "Beckham's Achilles' Tendon 'Totally Torn,' According to Surgeon," Goal: The *New York Times* Soccer Blog, March 14, 2010. goal.blogs.nytimes.com/2010/03/14/injured-beckham-may-miss-world-cup/.
24. Quoted in Rachel Rabkin Peachman, "Broken Bones and Bruises Rise and Youth Soccer Gets Aggressive," *New York Times*, September 13, 2016. www.nytimes.com/2016/09/13/well/family/broken-bones-and-bruises-rise-as-youth-soccer-gets-aggressive.html.

25. Quoted in Shailja Metha, "Reported Concussions in Youth Soccer Soar 1,600 Percent in 25 Years, According to Study," ABC News, September 12, 2016. abcnews.go.com/Health/reported-concussions-youth-soccer-soar-1600-percent-25/story?id=42030150.

Chapter 6: Technology in Soccer

26. Quoted in Jonas Dino and Jerry Colen, "NASA Turns World Cup into Lesson in Aerodynamics," NASA, July 30, 2015. www.nasa.gov/content/nasa-turns-world-cup-into-lesson-in-aerodynamics.
27. Quoted in Edgar Alvarez, "Nike's Latest Soccer Cleat Is Its Most Data-Driven Shoe Yet," Endgadget, July 25, 2016. www.engadget.com/2016/07/25/nike-magista-2-nsrl-inside-look/.
28. Quoted in Julie Foudy, "Sydney Leroux: Why Turf Is Terrible for Soccer Players," ESNPW.com, November 13, 2014. www.espn.com/espnw/news-commentary/article/11868149/sydney-leroux-explains-why-turf-terrible-soccer-players.
29. Quoted in Megan Logan, "The Wearable Prepping the US Women's Soccer Team for Battle," *Wired*, June 22, 2015. www.wired.com/2015/06/wearable-prepping-us-womens-soccer-team-battle/.
30. Quoted in Logan, "The Wearable Prepping the US Women's Soccer Team for Battle."

Glossary

anatomy: A branch of science that has to do with the structure of living things, especially the human body.

artificial intelligence (AI): A branch of computer science that deals with the simulation of intelligent behavior in computers.

central nervous system: The parts of the brain and spinal cord that receive and process stimuli from the body and coordinate appropriate physical responses.

dimensions: Mathematical measurements of the boundaries of an object or area.

electrode: A conductor used to establish electrical contact with a part of a circuit not made of metal.

endurance: The ability to tolerate difficult physical activity for a long period of time.

fatigue: The state of being very tired.

intravenous: Entering through a vein.

iterate: To say or do something more than once.

mass: The measurement of an object's size and how much material it contains.

molecule: The smallest particle of a substance that retains all the properties of that substance.

motion capture: Technology that digitally records specific movements and translates them into computer-animated images.

perimeter: The outer boundary of a geometric figure.

rehabilitation: The process by which a person is restored to health and activity.

scar tissue: The connective tissue that forms a scar.

stimulus: An event or condition in the environment that directly influences bodily activity in a living thing.

trajectory: The path of a moving object.

vestibular system: A system in the inner ear that is made up of three canals: the saccule, the utricle, and the semicircular canals.

For More Information

Books

Bodden, Valerie. *Soccer*. Mankato, MN: Creative Education, 2016.
This introduction to the physics of soccer provides basic examples of science concepts at work on the pitch.

Crawford, Andy, and Hugh Hornby. *Soccer*. New York, NY: DK, 2014.
This book, created in partnership with the National Football Museum in the United Kingdom, is a comprehensive overview of soccer—from its early history to its contemporary stars.

Goodstein, Madeline P. *Goal!: Science Projects with Soccer*. Berkeley Heights, NJ: Enslow Publishers, 2010.
This book includes science experiments that give the reader scientific insight into the physics of soccer.

Kortemeier, Todd. *Make Me the Best Soccer Player*. Minneapolis, MN: ABDO Publishing, 2017.
Readers discover how the best soccer players train to remain at the top of their game and find drills they can use to develop their own training programs.

Mahoney, Emily. *The Science of Soccer*. New York, NY: PowerKids Press, 2016.
Some of the most basic scientific principles that can be seen in action on the soccer field are simplified for readers in this introduction to the relationship between science and soccer.

Nagelhout, Ryan. *Talk Like a Soccer Player*. New York, NY: Gareth Stevens Publishing, 2016.
Nagelhout introduces readers to the basic terminology used by soccer players, coaches, and fans.

Peterson, Megan Cooley. *Wacky Soccer Trivia: Fun Facts for Every Fan.* North Mankato, MN: Capstone Press, 2017.
This book includes many pieces of fun trivia about soccer to enhance readers' knowledge of the sport.

Websites

FIFA
www.fifa.com
FIFA's official website features articles, scores, photos, and videos for both men's and women's matches.

"NASA Turns World Cup into Lesson in Aerodynamics"
www.nasa.gov/content/nasa-turns-world-cup-into-lesson-in-aerodynamics
This article gives a detailed description of the tests NASA ran on the Brazuca soccer ball and has a video of those tests being conducted by NASA engineers.

"The Power of Innovation—Creating Energy with Footsteps"
www.youtube.com/watch?v=EpYRH-njaAI
This YouTube video focuses on the development of and the reaction to the technology that has allowed the lights around soccer fields in developing nations to be powered by footsteps.

RoboCup
www.robocup.org
The official RoboCup website presents a detailed history of RoboCup, a complete list of leagues and events, and galleries featuring photos and videos of robotic soccer players in action.

Safety Tips: Soccer
kidshealth.org/en/teens/safety-soccer.html
This website provides important information on how to stay safe and avoid injuries while playing soccer.

U.S. Soccer
www.ussoccer.com

Soccer fans and aspiring superstars can read articles about, view schedules for, and see match results for the U.S. men's and women's national teams.

U.S. Youth Soccer
www.usyouthsoccer.org

Coaches and players in the U.S. Youth Soccer program can find valuable information on this website, including videos, guides, and online education courses on topics that range from concussions to nutrition.

Index

Picture Credits

Cover RichLegg/E+/Getty Images; cover, back cover, pp. 1, 3–4, 6, 18, 34, 48, 63, 77, 91, 94–95, 98, 103–104, (background) Ekaterina Koolaeva/ Shutterstock.com; pp. 4, 6, 18, 34, 48, 63, 77 (soccer ball) tmicons/ Shutterstock.com; p. 8 JIJI PRESS/AFP/Getty Images; p. 10 Matyas Rehak/ Shutterstock.com; p. 11 Rischgitz/Getty Images; p. 12 Popperfoto/Getty Images; pp. 14–15 Pictorial Parade/Archive Photos/Getty Images; p. 16 Ronald Martinez/Getty Images; p. 19 antpkr/Shutterstock.com; p. 21 Syda Productions/Shutterstock.com; p. 23 anek_s/iStock/Thinkstock; pp. 24–25 PHILIPPE DESMAZES/AFP/Getty Images; p. 26 Alesandro14/ Shutterstock.com; pp. 28–29 Gonzalo Arroyo Moreno/Getty Images; p. 32 Jefferson Bernardes/Shutterstock.com; p. 35 Stuart Franklin - FIFA/FIFA via Getty Images; p. 37 sciencepics/Shutterstock.com; p. 40 Joshua Weisberg/Icon Sportswire/Corbis via Getty Images; p. 42 (left) wavebreakmedia/ Shutterstock.com; p. 42 (right) Andrey_Popov/Shutterstock.com; p. 44 Laszlo Szirtesi/Shutterstock.com; p. 46 Alex Grimm/Bongarts/Getty Images; p. 50 mikkelwilliam/E+/Getty Images; p. 53 Rick Stewart/Allsport/Getty Images Sport/Getty Images; p. 54 gpointstudio/Shutterstock.com; pp. 56–57 Thomas Barwick/Iconica/Getty Images; p. 59 Jakkrit Orrasri/Shutterstock.com; p. 61 CHARLY TRIBALLEAU/AFP/Getty Images; p. 64 John Berry/Getty Images; p. 66 LDWYTN/Shutterstock.com; p. 68 Alila Medical Media/ Shutterstock.com; pp. 70–71 ANNE-CHRISTINE POUJOULAT/AFP/Getty Images; p. 73 Justin K. Aller/Getty Images; p. 75 GIUSEPPE CACACE/AFP/ Getty Images; pp. 78–79 courtesy of NASA's Ames Research Center; pp. 80–81 VCG/VCG via Getty Images; p. 84 Carmen Jaspersen/picture-alliance/dpa/AP Images; p. 86 EyesWideOpen/Getty Images; p. 88–89 YASUYOSHI CHIBA/AFP/Getty Images.

About the Author

Amy B. Rogers is an experienced nonfiction author who has written many books for young readers on topics that include American history, science, and women's participation in sports. She lives in a suburb of Buffalo, New York, with her husband, Steve, and their Welsh corgi, Jiminy.